CW00448364

Tim Krabbé

DELAY

*Translated from the Dutch
by Sam Garrett*

BLOOMSBURY

First published in Great Britain 2005

Originally published in Holland in 1994
by Uitgeverij Bert Bakker as *Vertraging*

The publishers gratefully acknowledge a
grant from the Foundation for the Production
and Translation of Dutch Literature.

Bloomsbury Publishing Plc, 38 Soho Square, London W1D 3HB

A CIP catalogue record for this book
is available from the British Library

ISBN 0 7475 7673 4
ISBN-13 9780747576730

10 9 8 7 6 5 4 3 2 1

Typeset by Hewer Text Ltd, Edinburgh
Printed in Great Britain by Clays Ltd, St Ives plc

All papers used by Bloomsbury are natural, recyclable
products made from wood grown in well-managed
forests. The manufacturing processes conform to the
environmental regulations of the country of origin.

DELAY

THIRTY AND A HALF years after he'd left Amsterdam on his moped for a camping holiday in Belgium and France, Jacques Bekker felt the Boeing-737 that was bringing him from Auckland to Sydney begin its descent. The coast of Australia came into sight, coves full of boats with unknown stories, and a little later the glistening peninsula of the city itself, with the giant arched bridge across the bay and the famous Opera House, sticking out into the water like a tray full of neat nuns' caps.

They were already past, and past the sea of houses, and on the rural side of Sydney the plane banked and began its final pass back toward the airport. Now level out, Jacques thought, and the plane did.

He set his watch back two hours: nine o'clock local time. Three hours ago in Auckland, at eight o'clock, his marathon across half the globe had begun. For almost a day and a half he and his companions would be sitting in planes and waiting in departure halls, and after a night which would be endless because they were following the sun, but too slowly, they would arrive in Amsterdam in the early morning. With a little luck he'd be home before seven. Then he would put down his suitcase, undress silently and crawl into bed beside Sonja, who was sleeping at his place for the occasion. It was winter in Amsterdam; the colder he'd be when he came in off the street, the more deliciously her warmth would seep through him when, still half asleep, she put her arms around him.

That she'd be leaving that same morning for a few days in Paris he saw as an elegant twist of fate. They'd have only a few hours together, but those hours, in which his journey became hers, would be apart from everything: nothing could happen to them.

Down below, a car was driving along a narrow road. Jacques watched it. That car was really there, but it seemed as though he could just as well be imagining it, as though you'd have to travel through time to get to that car. He would land in Sydney and leave it as if it was only an idea.

IN THE TRANSIT HALL, Jacques' group was herded together as much as possible by Marijke Eerhard, the representative from the ministry of culture who'd organized and supervised the trip. Two weeks of Dutch-language culture for Dutch emigrants in New Zealand: a film director, a columnist, a poet, an actress, a puppeteer. And a writer: Jacques Bekker. Eleven people, traveling partners included.

Jacques had loved the New Zealand air, more delicious to inhale than the most delicious cigarette he could remember, he'd loved his walks and the drives, the way everything was free and friendly, but also the awe in which he was held by the Dutch New Zealanders. They'd never heard of him, let alone read one of his books, but they treated him like a demi-god – which of course he was, as an emissary from the realm of their youth.

Not everyone saw it that way, though. Marijke Eerhard had actually reprimanded him for his 'rather frivolous attitude', but Jacques assumed that his audiences hadn't come for his views on literature, but for the illusion that they'd played hopscotch together on the same playground. And, in return for this wonderful junket, he had seen it as his duty toward those people living so far from their native soil to be their talking pair of wooden shoes.

Marijke announced that they had one hour to spare before the next leg to Singapore, and pointed out the spot where they would meet again. From Sydney they'd be flying Air India; so much for cultural budgets.

JACQUES HAD AN ESPRESSO with Anna Rector, the actress, then took a stroll past the duty-free shops. A little later, while he was poking around a newsstand, Anna came back to him to say that their flight had been delayed. Instead of at eleven, they'd now be leaving at three in the afternoon – a four-hour delay.

Monique, he thought, and a shiver ran through him.

Now he wouldn't get home until Sonja had already left. He felt tired suddenly, a failure, as if he'd never see her again, as if those couple of hours in bed together were what he needed not to have been lonely in New Zealand. He wanted to call her right away, and he could, because it wasn't even midnight in Holland, but Anna asked whether he felt like going into town. At least then they'd have some use for those visas for the cancelled Australian part of the tour. Edith Bolte, the director's wife, was coming too. She'd been in Sydney before, for a film festival, she could act as their guide. If all went well at customs, and at the taxi stand, they'd have two and a half hours in a faraway city; a way to kill time that didn't just drop into your lap every day.

Hans Bolte himself wasn't going, he wanted to stay

and work on a script. He'd keep an eye on the hand luggage.

THE TAXI DROPPED THEM off on a crowded shopping street amid skyscrapers, and there he was: Sydney. It was like he had performed magic by arriving in the droning, honking reality that he'd just seen lying silent and unreachable below.

They walked toward the center of town, and took each other's picture along a short, busy stretch of waterfront, Circular Quay, the place where the ferries moored. It was still before eleven, and Edith suggested taking the boat to Manly, where Sydney's huge bay opened on to the Pacific. It was a lovely, forty-five-minute trip, and in Manly they'd still have enough time to walk down the shopping street, stop for prawns and watch the surfers.

'I'm staying here,' Jacques said. And, when Anna looked at him in surprise: 'I'd rather lose my way.'

'So lose your way on the boat.'

'I'll wave to you.' And then, on impulse, he added: 'I have a demon to drive out.'

'Oh. Well, drive safely then.'

They agreed to look for each other along the quay at one o'clock. If they didn't meet up, they'd take separate cabs to the airport.

Jacques watched the two women until they were past the ticket office for the Manly ferry, and raised his hand when they looked around. He walked back down Circular Quay to the Opera House and climbed the broad stairs at the back where tourists lounged and took each other's pictures. Through a sort of alleyway between the nuns' caps he arrived at the water again. He discovered there was a sidewalk café there, with colorful parasols that tinkled in their standards in the cool breeze.

Leaning on the balustrade, he looked out across the sunny bay with its boats large and small, and its enormous bridge. After a while a ferryboat passed. A few little figures were waving, but it was too far away to pick anyone out. Just to be sure, he waved back.

He bought an ice-cream cone and watched the boat go. He thought about Monique. From the moment he'd heard about the delay, he'd known what he was going to do: go into Sydney and see if Monique Ilegems still lived there.

HE STARTED BACK TOWARD the center of town, looking for a public space where there might be a phonebook. A pub, preferably: he was thirsty, and the streets were getting hotter by the minute. This had to be the business district: fellows half his age, in serious neckties, were elbowing each other aside in the bustle amid the skyscrapers. And that at thirty-five degrees — a digital thermometer on the front of a department store told him so.

He didn't have Monique's address with him. Back when he'd still thought that they would be visiting Australia too, he had looked for it, but soon stopped with a vague feeling of irritation: ritualistic nonsense. It didn't matter anyway: he knew her name was now Monica George, her husband was Howard George. The street had some kind of weird German name; there was no way he could miss it.

The sheer thought that he might find Monique in a telephone book. Here, on the other side of the world!

But it had been at least eight years since he'd found the address, and who knows how long it might have been outdated even then. His letter had never gotten a reply. She might be long divorced, moved, dead. And in the unlikely event that she still lived at that address, then there wasn't much chance of her being at home. And if she was, and he rang the bell, and she opened the door – wouldn't she, as soon as he told her who he was, tell him to buzz off?

And if she asked him to come in . . .

Maybe that would be worst of all: the idea of talking over a cup of tea with a completely strange woman about something that had truly touched him, filled him with horror.

It didn't matter. Seeing a house where she'd once lived would be enough. One excuse to do something useless was as good as another, and if he could use Monique Ilegems, a lifetime after he'd seen her last, as the dice that determined what he got to see of an unknown city, then he had no reason to complain about her.

PAST THE TEAROOMS AND bodegas in the center he found a pub, in a gray building that looked like a parking garage. Inside it was cool and dark, and there were Australians drinking at the bar. Amid the bottles was a television set showing a horserace: the horses crossed the finish without anyone paying attention. The tables in the barroom were planks, fit high around poles that ran from floor to ceiling. Maybe this had been a fire station and the firemen had once slid down these poles.

With a big glass of beer and section A–K of the telephone book he'd borrowed at the bar, Jacques settled down on a barstool at one of the tables.

Just for fun, but also to pluck up the courage, he looked first under Ilegems. That name wasn't in it, so he leafed back to the G, to GE. He felt eyes turn on him from one of the other tables. A man and woman were sitting there, a cheerful-looking couple with bright tourist brochures in front of them; it wouldn't surprise him if they were Dutch.

It was like having her lay her hand on his arm. There it was, just like that: GEORGE Monica, 1 Leichhardt, Dlg. Pt. She jumped right out at him from the little half column of Georges.

Leichhardt, that was it. He put a check beside her name and looked at the date on the book: last year. There were two Howard Georges, both at different addresses.

And now: was he actually going to call?

The husband from the tourist couple got up and came over to him.

'Excuse me, are you by any chance Dutch?' he asked in English.

'Yes, I am,' Jacques said.

'Are you Jacques Bekker?'

'Yes.'

'So it *is* you! My wife said it was.' He waved and nodded to the woman, who smiled back, but seemed too shy to come over as well.

'There was this question in your quiz recently,' the man said. ' "A man's first name that is also a unit to measure weight?" The candidate said: "Gram", and you gave it to him. He was right, of course, but did you know that there's another correct answer?'

'Really?'

'Fulton. That's a measure of weight, too.'

9

'Well, I'll be damned,' Jacques said. The panel of experts of *WordCount*, the language quiz he hosted, had received more than a hundred letters with this alternative answer.

'On vacation?' the man asked. 'We just arrived, we'll be here for two months.'

'Yes, vacation.'

'But of course!' the man said, half-addressing his wife, as though he'd just made a discovery. 'Of course! You people go on vacation too!'

Jacques couldn't help laughing. 'I have to be going,' he said. 'The shooting for the new season starts in two days. My plane is leaving in a couple of hours and I'd like to feel that I'm really in Sydney for a little while still.'

The man nodded understandingly and, exactly because he didn't dare with these people watching, Jacques picked up the directory and carried it over to the phone. He punched in Monique's number, panicking only by the last digit at the thought that in one second he might be connected with her. It felt like he was holding a hot wire. There was an answering machine. A woman's voice, flat and businesslike, spoke the number he had just dialed, and asked him to leave a message or send a fax.

When the voice was over, he hung up. He had recognized nothing.

★   ★   ★

DLG. PT. WAS THE Darling Point district; on the way there, the taxi cut through a whole range of neighborhoods, each containing a possible course Monique's life could have taken. Where it stopped, that's how her life would have been: Jacques had absolutely no idea what had become of her.

The driver pulled over to the curb in a quiet, hilly neighborhood with capital villas and luxurious high-rise apartments, green everywhere and gorgeous views of the bay. Jacques had asked to be dropped at the corner, and when the taxi drove away he looked disbelievingly at the sign: LEICHHARDT STREET.

This was where the postman had walked to deliver his letter.

He had to suppress the urge to whistle through his teeth: Darling Point was for the rich. A sign indicated that Leichhardt Street came to a dead end, at the waterfront undoubtedly. The bay glistened through the branches of the trees, masts jutted up above their crowns.

He started walking downhill, along the even-numbered side of the street, his mouth dry with anxiety. Sturdy fences separated lawns from sidewalk. Someone, of whom all he could see was one dangling arm, was swaying gently in a hammock; in a driveway across the street a woman in a white dress was loading suitcases into a car; a little girl was pushing her bike uphill with both hands on the handlebars. Down below a rope tinkled through pulleys, a sail was being hoisted.

He was already at the waterfront, or rather, he saw that the driveway of the woman with those suitcases belonged to a ranch-style house that ran down to the water; there was a dock there with a few boats moored to it.

He stopped.

The woman glanced at him too, maybe his standing still had caught her eye. She bent over to a tube-shaped bag with the heads of golf clubs protruding from it.

In Jacques the thought arose that he could *make* her Monique Ilegems, out of nothing but his will that it was her and her presence in this street, where Monique had once lived. He crossed and walked up to her.

'Monique?' he said.

She looked up.

She was an attractive woman, he had already seen that in the way she moved, and now he was seeing it from close by. Fairly small, with something strong and resilient. Bare, tanned arms, small eyes, the mouth painted poppy red.

If it was her, then he was seeing her from unbelievably close by.

'Oh please,' she said. The voice of the answering machine, but impatient now, on the verge of annoyance.

'Do you recognize me?' he asked.

She looked. He'd said it in English, and he repeated it in Dutch.

Suddenly her face was alive.

'Jack,' she said. 'Jack, from Oppy's. Unbelievable.' She shook her head.

And he recognized her, or actually it was the other way around: it was as though he was back in Ostend, and from there was being allowed to look into this distant future. So this woman, with her chic white summer dress, who must be fifty or fifty-one, who had black hair instead of blonde, was playing the role of Monique Ilegems as older woman? But why not? She did look like her, like the photo from outside the casino.

He began saying something about his delay, but it was as though she didn't hear him.

'I always knew I'd see you again,' she said. 'But then today, of all days!'

'What's so special about today?' She'd kept speaking English, he switched back now too.

'Everything.' She laughed, a curt laugh that had something bitter to it.

'How are you doing?' he asked. 'Well, by the looks of it.'

She stared.

'Are you taking a trip?' he asked, nodding at the suitcases.

The question seemed to confuse her, as though she had to think about the answer. 'So you're here,' she said. 'Amazing. But I have to go. I've got an appointment. I'm sorry.'

I'm sorry – he saw the special significance of those words jump to her eyes. She smiled, her lips a crooked line. So she remembered that!

The smile faded. 'I have to go,' she said again. But she just stood there, sunk in some strange kind of trance, completely indecisive. Something unusual must have happened, right before he showed up.

'Or...no! Would you help me with something?' she said.

Jacques was already bending down to put the last suitcase in the car, expecting her to then slam the trunk, climb in and drive away, this time once and for all. But she put the suitcase in by herself, opened the passenger door for him, and a moment later Jacques Bekker had slid into an expensive sedan and was being driven by an elegant middle-aged woman along the lanes of Darling Point, Sydney.

So it *was* the right address, he thought.

THEY DROVE DOWN BROAD boulevards, away from her house, into new and unfamiliar neighborhoods. Jacques couldn't believe it was really Monique he was sitting beside. She stared straight ahead, her thoughts far away, with a brief, incredulous smile when he caught her eye.

The car phone rang; the sound made Jacques notice that she had one. She answered with a terse 'yes', and stuck for the rest to yeses and nos. It sounded like someone was giving her instructions. But by the end of the conversation Jacques had the impression that, against the other person's will, she had postponed an appointment until four-thirty that afternoon.

She hung up.

'So – Jack. Long time no see.'

'That's right.'

'What brings you here?'

'I came to see you.'

'To Australia?'

'No, no, this is a layover. My plane leaves at three.'

He looked at his watch: it was already past twelve-thirty. He'd never make the rendezvous at Circular Quay. She would just have to take him to the airport, that would be the easiest. He had already prepared the lightheartedness with which he would say goodbye: great to have seen you again.

'What kind of work do you do?' he asked. 'You certainly live in style.'

'Yes, I've made it. I'm a businesswoman.' She

laughed, that cynical little laugh again. 'A retired businesswoman. And you?'

'A writer.'

'I knew it.'

'You *knew* it?' He could see her in his mind's eye, in a
bookstore during a visit to Belgium, holding one of his
books, wondering whether this was the same Jacques
Bekker.

'Of course I did. Back then you said you wanted to be
a writer.'

'But that doesn't mean I became one, does it?'

'Oh yes it does, Jack. Oh yes. You can become
anything in life, as long as you want to.'

So you've become somebody with insights like that,
he thought. But still, she'd remembered, something from
so long ago.

The trance seemed over. Impatient and hectic now,
she talked on, racing from one subject to the next like
somebody who has to have a card stamped at check-
points, and then suddenly taken aback by her own self-
centeredness.

'Uh-oh, there I go again. Always talking about myself.
Tell me something about you.'

'My plane leaves at three.'

She looked at her watch. 'No problem. I'll get you
there.'

'I wrote you a letter once,' he said. 'Did you ever get it?'

'Yes.' A millionth of a gram of caution in her voice.

'Why didn't you write back?'

She shrugged. 'What could I have written − "*I'm sorry*"?'

'How should I know? The name of your dog.'

She looked at him. 'You're a crazy boy, Jack,' she said so suddenly in undiluted Flemish that he recognized her voice − and the phrase.

ANNA AND EDITH WITH their ferryboat couldn't hold a candle to this: an air-conditioned, chauffeur-driven tour of living, breathing, workaday Sydney. But it was a real scavenger hunt; Jacques could make no sense of the order in which residential neighborhoods, stretches of four-lane highway, shopping streets and industrial estates made way for the other.

Just when he was about to ask what she wanted him to help with, the phone rang again. With a gesture of annoyance, Monique flipped a switch and it was silent.

'Do you still live in Amsterdam?' she asked.

'Yes.'

'Married? Children?'

'No. And you?'

'Oh, divorced, two daughters, twenty-four and twenty-two. Do you have a girlfriend?'

'Yes.'

'How long have you been together?'

'Almost a year.'

'How old?'

'Twenty-seven.'

'That's young. Jack, I'm going to be frank with you. You arrived at a very strange moment. I'm in trouble, big trouble. You have to help me.'

'Okay.'

'But what I need you to do must remain a secret.'

'Will anyone be in danger if I do?'

'*I'll* be in danger if you don't.'

THEY HAD STOPPED ALONG a broad street, lined with low houses on the other side, stores on theirs. Monique had said she needed time to think; she was staring straight ahead, her hands on the wheel. At the traffic light further along was a theater or sports hall with a sign announcing a boxing match at an hour when they would have long gone their separate ways. Jacques wanted to know what the street was called, so he could find it again later on a map. This was part of it now, too: Ostend-Brussels-Sydney.

'Can you drive?' she asked.

'Sure.'

'Good. Then we're going to Parramatta Road.' She started the car and drove off.

Now Monique drove straight where she wanted to go, and a few minutes later they were on a scorched, stinking six-lane road. The dilapidated factories and low white houses on both sides were punctuated by brightly colored neon signs that looked like they belonged in front of gambling palaces: this was Parramatta Road. The signs were the exclamation marks indicating pennant-hung lots full of used cars, the prices smeared across their windshields in big white numbers. The sun sparkled on hoods and in countless mirrors.

Just past a sign saying CEDRICS BEST MOTORS, VALUE PRICED CARS, Monique turned into a side street. She stopped, opened her purse, and before Jacques knew what was happening he had a pile of banknotes in his hand, hundred-dollar bills. He looked at it with a mixture of distaste and awe, the same feeling he'd had the time someone sitting next to him had suddenly taken a shot of heroin.

'Here's ten thousand dollars,' Monique said. 'Buy the best Ford Falcon you can get for that money. A Ford Falcon.'

'Why don't you do it yourself?'

'I'm pretty well known in Australia, Jack. I don't want anyone to see me with that car. You said you were going to help me, right? I'll wait here. As soon as I see you coming I'm going to drive away, and you'll follow me.'

DIZZY FROM THE GLEAMING sun – it must have been forty degrees out – and the beer, Jacques walked around the corner to Cedric's Motors, her presumptuous money in his pocket. He was too baffled to be angry. The enormity of the cash he'd seen in her bag, bundles of banknotes with rubber bands around them, large and small, stuffed in hastily, was like a defect she'd shown him, a plea for consideration. People who carried that much money around, maybe there was something wrong with them, maybe other laws applied to them.

But still: she was using him. Just like back then. Unbelievable: these were the few minutes they had together after thirty years – and she was sending him on an errand.

He looked at his watch: a few minutes past one. Edith and Anna were probably already back at Circular Quay and looking for him now. He was actually starting to feel a little anxious. He had no idea how far it was from here to the airport, but Sydney could never be so big that you couldn't make it in forty-five minutes. If worst came to worst, two-thirty might still be okay. He could already

20

see Marijke Eerhard stamping her feet in concern. 'Sorry, Marijke, I had to stop in and buy a car.'

CEDRIC, A LEBANESE IN a dustcoat, had a Ford Falcon for 9,975 dollars, only five years old and ideal for the open road. But while they were walking toward it, Jacques' eye was caught by a station wagon with a long, broad hood, elegant as a cheap toy car and sprayed such a bright orangeish-red, with beautiful black stripes, that he asked what kind that was – a Ford Falcon, for 7,750 dollars. He took it right away, with the pleasant feeling that he was cheating Monique by saving her 2,250 dollars.

He turned down the offer of a test drive. While a young boy washed the price off the windshield, he paid and took the papers, and less than ten minutes after walking in he was driving off the lot, around the corner to Monique. She should be glad he hadn't bought a motorbike.

SHE WAS WAITING ON the sidewalk, leaning against her car. She gave him the thumbs-up, climbed in and started driving: a commanding black car with the license MAD 20. The blue-tinted back window made her invisible, like a head of state in a passing motorcade. Jacques followed thirty meters behind her.

And now: in convoy to the airport. This drive, in

separate cars, would have to be the conclusion of what their lives had to do with each other. But it *was* a real stroke of luck, getting to drive a Ford Falcon like this one, not at all like the little Datsuns he'd rented in New Zealand, or his Citroën in Amsterdam. A front seat that could hold four, as long as a battle-cruiser, you rolled down the road like you were crossing a calm sea, you could feel the horsepower under you, straining at the bit to show what it could do. It had a radio, too. Jacques pushed a button and a pounding rock song washed over him.

He rolled down the window and leaned his elbow on the sill.

I'm driving on the left, and I'm doing it perfectly, he thought. What an adventure: instead of dozing away in some departure hall, thinking up questions for his quiz, or going for a ferry ride, he was King of the Road in a Red Shark in Sydney.

But after a while he began to realize that what made his expert left-hand driving so striking was precisely all the turning, braking and crossing he had to do. There was no end to the scrawl of melting side streets in this part of Sydney, which was definitely not in any tourist guide; Monique seemed unable to find Parramatta Road again, or any other through street. How on earth could this be the fastest way to the airport?

But had they really agreed to go there? Suddenly, the moment she'd actually said that was nowhere to be found. 'Follow me,' was what she'd said. What could she possibly do on her own with two cars at the airport? The Ford Falcon had to be dropped off somewhere first, only then would she have time to take him.

'Quarter to two,' the disc jockey said. Quarter to two – and they hadn't gone anywhere! At three o'clock his plane would leave – it would fly *away*. And she was just driving around!

He turned off the radio, in order to concentrate on his anxiety.

She was making him transport drugs. What else would a woman like her be doing in a neighborhood like this? Her agitation, her 'trouble', the help he had to give. She was obviously filthy rich, with her house on the bay, that car, that insane bag of money. That 'retired business-woman', that 'today of all days', that jittery manner – had something gone wrong? Was she trying to cut her losses at a single shot, like that American automobile tycoon a few years back? The order for 'a Ford Falcon for ten thousand dollars', was that some kind of password, had Cedric told someone to put the stuff in the car while he was paying? If he got pulled over, she could drive on, free as a bird, and he would spend years behind bars. And when they finally found the spot where the Ford Falcon

23

was to be dropped, she'd leave him in the lurch, and he could forget all about catching his plane. No: he'd seen too much already, he'd be taken somewhere and rubbed out.

That last thought calmed him down again, because it couldn't be true. He looked for the horn, couldn't find it, cursed and slammed the steering column and found it by accident: a strangled sound that wouldn't even reach her car cruising imperturbably ahead. And what if he suddenly shot into a side street and ditched her? Not a chance: he'd still be caught in this web of side streets by the time the others had reached Singapore.

He hit the gas, passed her and braked. He heard her tires squeal on the asphalt and felt her bumper hit his. Glass tinkled, on the sidewalk two boys stopped and looked. With one giant step he was out of the Ford Falcon and standing beside her car. Her window buzzed open.

'I'm going to miss my plane! Goddammit, Monique! What are you doing?'

He was startled by her look: a child about to be abandoned at a dreaded summer camp.

'You said you were going to help me.'

'With what?'

'I'm trying to disappear.'

★   ★   ★

A LITTLE FURTHER ALONG, Monique found what she must have been looking for the whole time: a deserted little street where the cars rested on crates instead of on wheels, and with little gardens like the bottoms of drained canals, so full of hopeless garbage. She stopped beside a fence where the overhanging tree branches formed a tunnel of shadow, and Jacques stopped behind her.

In a few moves both cars were open and her impeccable suitcases had been tossed into the Falcon. She held out her hand for the keys, hesitated for a moment, then threw her own keys in through the open window of her car. She climbed behind the wheel of the Falcon, rolled up the window, turned on the air-conditioning and pulled away from the curb.

EURELLA STREET, Jacques read on the street sign.

'Your seatbelt,' she said.

The car rustled with a pleasant coolness.

NOW MONIQUE FOUND THE boulevards without a detour and signs for the airport soon appeared, but the first one said it was still twenty kilometers away. It would have been more help if it had said how many traffic lights remained, they were all red anyway, and the road was smothered with butting trucks; Marijke Eerhard had been walking around wringing her hands for at least half an hour now. But Monique refused to drive any faster than eighty, the limit.

'You can go past him, come on, I'm going to miss my plane!'

She looked at her watch. 'I think you're right, Jack.'

'Let *me* drive!'

'No. It's a miracle that you came. That you came today. I want to get everything I can out of that miracle. Without taking you into account. Okay?'

'Just like back then.'

'Oh no,' she said, touching his arm lightly. 'No, Jack. What I did then was the worst thing I've ever done.'

'I have to be in the studio on Thursday. I'm well known too. I've got a TV show about language.'

'Thursday? Today's Tuesday. And Europe's half a day behind. If you miss your plane, I'll buy you a new ticket. Business class.'

'That doesn't go any faster.'

'That depends. Which airline are you flying?'

'Air India.'

'Air India!' She laughed. 'People who fly Air India, well, I actually don't associate with them. Listen, Jack. If you want to get to Amsterdam on time, you know what you need to do? Miss that plane.'

And while Jacques was thinking that, with her ticket, he could not only beat his own plane home, but actually make up for his whole delay and maybe even be in time to crawl into bed with Sonja after all, she added: 'But why don't you come with me instead?'

At ten to three, the Ford Falcon pulled up to the sidewalk in front of the departure hall. They kissed, and Jacques jumped out of the car and ran off. She shouted something he couldn't hear. Time was up, he couldn't ask her anymore.

There were lines at both passport control counters. He got in the shorter one, and at the very moment he located the big flight information board his own flight changed from final call to departed.

He stepped out of line and cut to the customs desk. Behind him he heard protests, and his path was suddenly blocked by a man with a walkie-talkie who wanted to know where he thought he was going. Three o'clock? – then his plane was taxiing down the runway right now. He'd have to go to the Air India counter to find out what to do.

When Jacques turned around he saw Monique, half hidden behind a newspaper kiosk by the entrance. She held her hands up questioningly. He shook his head and went to her. And now he should have said something about that ticket she'd promised, or else she should have. But neither of them said a thing. Monique started walking, and he followed her, through the sliding glass doors, out of the hall, into the blazing heat of the day.

The red Ford Falcon was waiting at the curb.

Jacques held his breath – he couldn't believe he was walking along, that neither of them were saying anything, that he opened the door, climbed into the car.

Monique started the engine and pulled away.

It was as though he had boarded a ship that was sailing out of a harbor.

MONIQUE LEFT THE AIRPORT behind, moved into normal traffic, and soon they were driving down boulevards where not a single car had anything to do with the airport. Jacques leaned back, speechless at the mad intervention he was allowing her to make in his life. One word, one thought would be enough to stop what was happening here, but he wasn't capable of it. He wondered when it had been decided that he, standing on the sidewalk beside the open door of the Ford Falcon, would climb in. Before she had said: come with me. Before he'd seen her again at Darling Point. It had already been decided the first time he saw her, when she was twenty, at Oppy's in Ostend, standing at the edge of the dance floor.

'Did you make me miss my plane on purpose?' he asked.

She looked back at him, wise and naughty. 'Yes.'
'You just do whatever you want.'
'I just do whatever *you* want.'

THE SEA OF HOUSES thinned out, even the remotest suburbs of immeasurable Sydney were behind them now, and in the distance there appeared ranges of hills and mountains. The Blue Mountains, Monique said, the convicts who had lived here two centuries ago had thought China lay on the other side.

The Ford Falcon spread its wings. Cedric had been right: this was a car made for broad horizons. They tore across the blue mountains, then Monique headed in a more southerly direction, through forests, bare red land-scapes where lonesome trees stuck out of the ground like witches' hands, along dusty roads where stones clattered against the bottom of their car. The sky was deep blue, with little, shiny white clouds.

She asked whether he felt like driving, but he quickly said no. To drive the Ford Falcon again, he'd like nothing better, but to have a steering wheel in his hands now . . . he'd be forced to have a will, and then the only thing he could do would be to say that this had been going on long enough, and turn around on the spot. What was happening now had to go on happening, and while it was happening he'd look out the window, like a paralyzed king being shown the newest landscapes.

A peace Jacques didn't understand seemed to have descended over Monique – he'd seen her leave a very expensive car behind for all comers, and now she was driving this old heap along as though a burden had been lifted from her shoulders. Four-thirty was approaching, but she seemed to have forgotten all about her appointment, and nothing rose up from the landscape that she could possibly be heading for.

The disc jockey *said* it: four-thirty. He looked at her, and she looked back.

'Not going to your appointment?'

'No.'

'Why not?'

'Change of plans.'

'What's going on?'

'Ever heard of Madame Twenty?'

The name did ring a bell, like something endlessly faraway, like the names of your childhood pets – but at the same time close by.

'Isn't that T-shirts and things?'

He remembered now – at the airport he had seen a Madame Twenty shop.

Monique laughed. 'A bit more than just that, Jack.' Madame Twenty, that was the name of her company, that was how she herself was known. Madame Twenty ladies' and girls' sportswear, recreational and jogging clothes, accessories, Madame Twenty perfumes. It had started in Sydney, twenty-five years ago, and now she was all over Australia and New Zealand, and even in Japan a little, with her own factories in Seoul and Madras. Thirty-eight hundred employees, it had just kept growing. In fact, Madame Twenty was now a whole string of companies. 'They also do a lot of business between them, and Jack – it seems they're not always completely straightforward about that.'

The police were looking for her, maybe not today, but by tomorrow or the next day for sure. For a moment she'd thought *he* was a policeman, or a journalist. Ten minutes before he arrived at her house she'd received a tip-off that her bookkeeper was going to talk, she didn't have a day to spare. She would get at least three years in prison, and besides: her business career was over, forever. That was a pity, but in life you win some and you lose some, and today would be the first day of the rest of that life. She had seven hundred and eighty thousand dollars on her; that should keep her going for a while.

KATOOMBA, OBERON, SHOOTERS HILL, Taralga: place names that, if you saw them on a map, would drive you wild with curiosity about all the little things that went on there. Now he *was* there, but instead of drinking cold beer on the roofed porch of a pub, they raced through – as long as she still looked like Madame Twenty, Monique didn't want to get out of the car.

When she spotted the ruins of a house a ways off the road, she drove to it across the open field. Carrying a suitcase, she disappeared behind a wall and came back a little later wearing old sneakers, a pair of cut-off jeans, a plain red T-shirt, sunglasses and a cap that said BUNGAN BEACH SURF LIFESAVING CLUB. The make-up was gone from her face.

'Good thing I'm so beautiful,' she said. 'If I don't want to be recognized, all I have to do is make myself ugly.'

AT A SUPERMARKET IN Goulburn, they did some shopping. It was amazingly, miraculously exciting, whenever they'd lost each other amid the maze of racks and shelves, to suddenly see her pop up again in the next aisle. They tossed everything they saw into their cart, money was no object. And whatever one of them chose, the other approved. Cooled beverages, a pineapple, a bottle of peroxide and bleaching powder, roadmaps, beaded seat-covers to keep from sticking to the vinyl, a cooler, shaving gear, T-shirts that had been waiting for very different people. But the extra package of razors Jacques tossed into their cart had suddenly halted in midair.

Razors: he already had those, didn't he? High above the Australian continent, already on their way to Amsterdam?

The razors fell. And Monique nodded to him: good idea.

THE RADIO PLAYED, THE heat faded, the light faded, they were approaching the sea. Occasionally they smiled at each other, like two wise caterpillars about to spin their cocoons. Jacques was keeping an eye out for his first kangaroo; according to Monique, they came out at dusk. But probably not here, in the inhabited coastland. In Darling Point there were koala bears, she often found them in her garden.

Maybe it was all very simple, this reckless lethargy of his. This day would come to an end. What would that end look like? A motel room, together? What would it be like in that room? He couldn't summon up a picture in his mind – he wished he was already there, so reality could help him out a little.

THEY HAD REACHED THE coast again at Batemans Bay, a little port on the Pacific a few hundred kilometers south of Sydney. A river emptied into the ocean there, and between its banks was a long bridge, barely wide enough for two cars to pass because of a narrow walkway on the ocean side. The night was dark and clear, its sky so thick with stars that it looked like someone had splattered paint. Small groups of talkers leaned over the railing and dropped cigarette butts into the water, two Aborigines were gesticulating vehemently at each other, an angler was still angling. From behind Jacques' back came the occasional hissing of a car, absorbed each time by the evening sounds of Batemans Bay: the voices on the bridge, the distant put-putting of boats, the lapping of the waves against a piling, faint music from both far shores. Its mast lowered, a little sailboat was motoring under the bridge, an old man silent at the helm, his wife on a bench across from him. Jacques waved; surprised, they waved back.

The two black men were deaf and dumb, Jacques saw now, their gestures were sign language. It was ten o'clock, and still warm. He was completely happy.

But at the start of the bridge there had been a telephone booth, and he had walked past it. Two steps, a door, a couple of numbers and he would have been connected with the Institute for Physical Geography in Amsterdam, and with Sonja. In Goulburn she had gotten out of bed, in Doughboy she'd arrived at the institute, and later, when it was night here, she would bike to his house – for nothing, because she'd wake up in his bed without him having arrived. He had to prevent that, and

34

he wanted to, but the inexplicableness of what had happened to him kept him from doing it.

He started back. Monique would be ready by now; she'd said she needed an hour and a half to cut and bleach her hair. At the end of the bridge that telephone booth was there again, and again he walked past it. It was none of Sonja's business that he was in Batemans Bay, that he'd leaned over the railing of a bridge and looked at the water.

It was no one's business.

He stuck his hand in his pocket, and felt a warm roll of paper. Money, gone limp with his own sweat, the money left over from buying the Ford Falcon. Twenty-two hundred and fifty dollars, he'd forgotten all about it. He put it in his back pocket and buttoned the flap.

There was no one on the sidewalk on the ocean side, and no one on the beach either. From the pubs across the road came music and laughter, but you could also hear the rustle and sweep of waves across the beach. At great intervals there were lampposts with round caps, spreading a grayish, bluish light.

It was as though he'd landed in one of the dreams he called his blue dreams. He'd had no more than five or six of them in his whole life. They were always set in this very same light, and nothing ever happened in them, always the same nothing. He was alone, and he was walking up to a house where there might be a woman, who might be his lover. That was all, but the uncertainty of what would happen was divinely exciting; a bliss that couldn't be compared to anything in normal life, and the feeling of happiness those dreams left behind was un-bearable, almost painful, a pain that only ebbed away days later.

And, at the same time, this was his old fantasy about Monique. She was sorry, she'd dug up his address and involved his mother, later his friends, in a plot to get into his room, and now she was lying in his bed, waiting for him.

Past a bend he saw the purple neon letters of their motel. Even from here he could pick out the Ford Falcon, big and long in the gloom. In the motel parking lot he stopped. Everything was silent. What did he really know about her? – nothing. Only that her life, the way it had been between then and now, had today come to an end. Her cheerfulness of the last few hours could be the flush of collapse. She had a pistol, full of bravura she'd shown it to him when she emptied her bag on to the bed. She was fifty; suddenly she might have seen the second-handedness, the tawdriness of the new life she'd been trying to conjure out of her box of blonde hair coloring.

★   ★   ★

SHE HAD CUT THE pineapple into chunks and filled a plate for each of them, with cocktail picks. She was fresh, new, just born, in blue jeans and a T-shirt with a shark on it, and with a boyish, feathered, orange-blonde haircut that could have come straight from the girl of Ostend. The television was on, she was watching it cross-legged from the head of the double bed. When the pineapple was finished, she jumped up limberly, pulled on her sneakers and said: 'Come on, let's go eat. I'm dying of hunger.'

IT WAS A MIRACLE: he had been afraid that she'd run him out of her street, and now she stuck her arm through his, hopped once to match his step, and looked up at him as though they were two kids skipping school. Jacques thought about his traveling companions. They must be in Singapore by now, Anna and Edith at the center of attention. How had he acted? Did they have any idea what might have happened? Where *was* he? But no matter how hard they tried to imagine him, they could never see him here, a warm evening breeze brushing his temples, the hissing of the sea in his ears, Monique Ilegems on his arm.

HE'D EXPECTED HER TO try to keep a low profile, but it seemed as though Monique wanted to put her disguise to the test: *she* asked passers-by about restaurants, and at those restaurants, which were all full, she asked how long it would take before there would be a table. The wait was always too long for her; at a food counter, they bought pizza and boxes of salad to take to a pub. That's how it went in Australia: in restaurants you could bring your own wine, in pubs your own food, and millionaires ate pizza. The man behind the bar even had some cutlery for them.

The pub had a garden that faced the river, with strings of colored lights between the trees, and little tea-lights on the tables. Around them, the drinking and talk was subdued, and from an adjoining hall came soft music. If Monique was really so famous, then she'd certainly disguised herself well: no one looked at her for more than a second.

They were quiet.

'I did start to write you a letter then,' she began suddenly. It was like he was finding that letter in his mail, now.

'What did it say?'

'Dear Jack.'

'And then?'

'Then I didn't know what else to say.'

'Good letter. You should have sent it like that.'

'Yes, maybe I should have.'

'Hotel Memlinck has been torn down, did you know that?'

'Hotel Memlinck?'

'The hotel where you stayed.'

'That dump! They should have torn it down back then.' But again he saw the wariness behind her big talk.

'Have you ever been back to Ostend?' he asked.

'No.'

'I have. Often.'

'Why?'

'Yeah, why? I don't know. To see if maybe time had made a mistake and it was still that summer when you came.'

'And? Did I come?'

'Yes.'

'You have to live ahead, Jack, not backwards.' But he saw that he'd whisked her back to Ostend too, and in him the breathtaking thought arose that there was no hurry, that if he wanted he had more than just this evening to find out everything.

The pizzas were finished, the music from the hall grew louder, and when they went to look it turned out there was a disco that night. Jacques didn't like to dance, and knew he did so poorly, but he let himself be swept along by Monique. And for once it was as though his brusque, stiff movements were elegant, in keeping with the way

39

this insane day should go. It was still the same day! – the day that had started in New Zealand with fried eggs at breakfast in a hotel, and now he was dancing like mad in Batemans Bay, somewhere on the Australian coast. It was as though he'd been sucked in by a wheel of fortune, and spat out on this spot.

Between numbers they drank beer at the bar. A tall man and his redheaded wife, the only other people their age who were dancing, came over to them.

'Good for the old bones, this music!' the man shouted. 'Rattle 'em around a bit!'

His name was Ken, his wife was Gail, Monique was Paula.

'Paul,' Jacques said before he knew it.

'Paul and Paula!' Gail said. 'How cute!'

'But also a real pain,' Monique said. 'When I call him, I'm the one who comes!'

Song after song they danced, and everyone looked at Monique, who danced exuberantly but at the same time tightly, like a child who crayons in wild colors but stays between the lines – but people also looked at the two of them together: the other dancers, the disc jockey, the people around the dance floor. And through all the numbers and all the beats, her sentence pounded in Jacques' head: 'I'm trying to disappear.' The guts that took! The shock of exhilaration that had run through him when he heard himself use another name, for the first time in his life. This wasn't just a dance of joy, a mating dance – it was a vanishing dance. Missing a plane, Sonja, his quiz: it didn't mean a thing. To really vanish, to never let anyone hear from you again, to celebrate your birthday in a godforsaken desert instead of at some chic party, that was what she was offering him by dancing the way she danced – and that was what he was going to do.

2

T HEY REACHED OSTEND on the second day, the moped made it without a hitch. Beside the campground was a soccer field, and as soon as they'd pitched their tent an evening game began. Peter didn't like soccer, but Jacques jumped across a little ditch and watched. The final score was 3–1, and never again would there be a 3–1 that didn't bring back a waft of that summer evening – and of Monique.

When the game was over, night fell. They went into town and ended up on a long street paved with gray cobblestones that was, appropriately enough, called Langestraat. It was crowded and fun there, with little groups of boys and girls, cars that people climbed out of, and everywhere the sound of top twenty hits from Radio Luxembourg: Frankie Avalon, Lloyd Price, Brenda Lee, Paul Anka. There were snack bars, movie theaters and cafés door-to-door, dance clubs without a cover charge or doormen who checked to see whether you were old enough. At a corner they went into one: a low, white building with a lonely glass awning above the door.

It was dark inside. In a corner, on a little podium, a jukebox was playing a slow song. A mirror ball on the ceiling speckled the motionless couples on the floor with spots of light that crawled over their clothing like white butterflies. Peter asked a girl to dance, Jacques just stood and watched. The room was filled with unspeakable promise, and he knew he would have to come back here until it was clear what that promise was.

The place was called Oppy's, he saw once they were outside.

The next day they rode on to France.

3

THERE WAS NO kiss, no embrace, before they went to bed. And even there they looked at each other first, in the dim light from outside, a little space in between them, leaning on elbows, silent, smiling as though at some stupid misunderstanding, still tired from dancing.

Later, when they made love, Jacques was amazed at his own calm, at the proficiency with which he moved in her, the deliberation with which he postponed his own climax and then roused his lust again by looking at her face, 'the face of a woman fucking'. As if it was about increasing his pleasure, or hers. This was Monique! And while he was noticing an awkwardness in her movements that he wouldn't have expected, and that touched him, he realized with a start that he no longer remembered what it had been like in Ostend. Recalled to a pulp, probably, gone to story: the moped ride to Hotel Memlinck, the fire escape, the lights of ships at sea. Still, without recognizing anything in particular, he recognized: images he sniffed up from her neck, and that must have been waiting there all this time to be remembered by him now, but were hidden irretrievably in a smell.

It was a momentous occasion, momentous because of the fucking, but almost too momentous for fucking.

HE WOKE UP WITH the thought that *WordCount* was still within reach. The evening before, while looking around for a restaurant, he'd also seen a travel agency. Perhaps there was even an airfield at Batemans Bay. Within a few hours he could be on his way.

While Monique was busy packing, he went outside. Beside the Ford Falcon he stopped, his hand on the roof. He had everything he needed. His passport, the money left over from the car. He could just keep walking, down the boulevard, hail a cab. When she came outside he'd be gone. She'd call his name, look for him, but she'd know right away what had happened: he had given her a taste of her own medicine.

How could he decide? She might be finished any minute. It was like two continents drifting apart, and he had only this moment to decide which one to step on to.

Come on, here I go, he thought, and started walking, but he walked toward the lobby. On the sidewalk in front of the little office was a newspaper rack, and he took a paper.

Almost a quarter of the front page was taken up by a photo of Monique.

He had a book of fairy tales in his hand – a book he had to enter.

THE EAST COAST CURVED around to south coast, New South Wales became Victoria, the weather changed. Without stopping they drove through Melbourne, where the skyscrapers were fuzzy like photos behind a flyleaf. The second night they spent in Geelong, a town a hundred kilometers further along the bay; the next morning it rained there. They bought umbrellas and sweaters, and drove toward the Southern Ocean, through flat and lonely countryside with narrow roads where only the occasional tractor crept along, slow and crooked as a fly through a puddle of beer. Jacques saw his first kangaroo, in broad daylight, a soggy creature that came skipping laboriously across the road and made for the shelter of the woods. The radio was full of the coldest January day in Victoria in the one hundred and thirty years since they'd started keeping track – and of the fall of Madame Twenty.

A warrant for her arrest had been issued.

High along the edge of the cliffs, the coast road offered

terrifying panoramas out across the gray, bucking ocean, then ran down so low and close that it looked like they were driving straight through the surf. And then they rose again and saw the whole sea. Never had Jacques seen water so heavy, so formidable.

At a panoramic viewpoint they got out. As soon as she opened it, Monique's umbrella unfolded into a helpless black tulip. She threw it in a trash can and danced off through the rain, her arms in the air, springing and shrieking through the puddles. It took a few moments before Jacques heard that she was yelling words: 'I'm Madame Twenty! I'm Madame Twenty, here I am! Catch me if you can!'

He shouted to her to stop, but she kept screaming, and he couldn't hold back his own laughter.

They leaned over the railing, wet to the bone, and looked down at the waves ramming the cliff. The water spouted up like bombs were being dropped in it. The granite all along the bottom had been washed away; in caves and beneath natural bridges the sea stomped dull and gurgling. The remains of former cliffs stood upright like broken bottles in the sea, foam blowing all around them. In a few hours they'd start the shooting of *WordCount* – the thought made Jacques shiver with pleasure, and blew away a moment later like a toffee wrapper in the wind.

Beside the parking lot was a little graveyard, with wooden crosses and the names of infants and sea captains who had been swallowed up here a hundred years ago by the beastly waves; Jacques was amazed that bodies could even be recovered along a coast like this.

'Fantastic surfing here!' Monique shouted.

'Whaat?'

'Fantastic surfing!'

'You do that too?' He had to roar between the thunderclaps, she roared back.

'All Australians surf. I've got a team. Had a team.'

She stuck her hand in with his in the pocket of his brand-new jacket, and pointed with her other hand at the graves.

'You know how many ships have wrecked here? Five hundred!'

'What?'

'Five hundred ships wrecked here. Some surf!' Suddenly she pressed herself against him, her arms under his jacket. 'Oh Jack. Oh Jack. Say something sweet to me.'

He had been searching for something that could express his ridiculous joy at just being able to see her, but her request swept it all away. He threw his arms around her: a funny, windblown little lady who was turning to him for shelter, and who, according to the *Sydney Morning Herald*, the *Adelaide Advertiser* and the

Melbourne Age, had absconded with sixty-eight million dollars, eleven million of which through a sophisticated subsidy scam that had left four hundred families in Cabramatta without jobs.

BY HUNDREDS, THOUSANDS, THE kilometers spun away on the odometer of the red Ford Falcon. Day in, day out, their goal was to reach a spot they'd picked out on the map in order to have a goal – and to stay out of the hands of the police until the Madame Twenty affair had blown over enough to leave Australia safely.

She was Paula Fuerst from Adelaide now, forty-two years old; she'd wanted the age on her new ID to be as inconspicuous as possible. She wore her glasses, her now genuinely blonde spiked hair, her floral shorts and Madame Twenty T-shirts with such conviction that it truly made her a different person from the worldly, elegant Madame Twenty.

Jacques changed too. There were plenty of Dutch tourists in Australia, and it wouldn't be long before there were Dutch people who knew about his disappearance and were keeping an eye out for him. In order not to endanger Monique, he had to be able to travel around freely as well, and so he wore sunglasses and a necklace, a hat, he let his beard grow and had her shave his head. After making a few calls he acquired, on a surprisingly middle-class street in Adelaide, the passport of Leslie Elder, aged forty-nine, of Cessnock, New South Wales, for eight thousand dollars and a photo.

They slept in motels, bought a tent so they could stay at campgrounds too, always under different names, and never remained anywhere longer than a night. It might have been safer in the big cities, but it was as though their journey had to be this journey, music blasting in the Ford Falcon, following red sand tracks lined with kangaroo carcasses, through garishly lush valleys and Wild West towns with left-hand traffic, past the spot where a camel driver had been shot dead because he'd washed his feet in a spring for drinking water, past eucalyptus forests, vineyards, a tractor built in 1920 that still worked, a sign for a town reading 'Pop. 4' where the 4 had been crossed out by hand and replaced with a 5.

But above all, they passed through terrifying emptiness: plains so endless that driving didn't change a thing. One day, soaked with sun and kilometers, Jacques opened the door to climb out and Monique grabbed his arm and pulled him back: they were still driving. Because of the driving, always driving, it was impossible to remember *that* they were driving.

IT'S MONIQUE, HE KEPT thinking. It really is Monique. It is unbelievable. And then he looked over and saw beside him, in the Ford Falcon, in bed, on the path they walked, the attractive middle-aged woman who went with him and loved him with an obviousness bordering on the blunt, the only person in the world who could clarify what had gotten into Monique Ilegems thirty years ago.

She didn't want to talk about it.

'Leave those two fools alone, Jack. It's not fair, they can't defend themselves. We were too young.'

'And now we're too old.'

'You're never too old.'

'Not even to start a family?'

'Not for life. We know what life is now.'

'Yeah, almost finished.'

'No, Jack! For us it's just starting. Back then it was easy to fall in love, things that are still unformed will always fit together. But now we have a life, now things don't just fit like that. When we're in love now, it's worth something.'

'So you're old enough for love once you're too old for it. That's nonsense. Love is for those who don't know anything about it.'

And then she would be silent, staring straight ahead in disappointment. But another good mood was never long in coming. The crowbar hadn't been made that could pry the two of them apart.

51

She gave him the full brunt of her love. It was baffling: she'd once tossed him aside with unforgettable viciousness, and now she bought a nice little picture frame to stick a Polaroid of the two of them to the dashboard. He had only to wonder out loud what a bird was called, and there was a hundred-dollar photo book of *Birds of Australia* on the backseat. She bought an *Encyclopedia of World Literature*, and was disappointed when she didn't find his name in it: 'Stupid book.' She always wanted to make love, and she always came, quickly and with a little sound as though she'd suddenly heard of a calamity. When they went to sleep afterwards, she demanded that he curl up against her, his chest to her back, his knees against the back of hers, and she took his hand and put it around her lower breast. Sometimes, when conversation lulled, she'd look at him and say: 'Say something sweet to me.' Jacques never knew what to do, until he hit upon the idea of replying with 'something sweet to me'; to his relief, she accepted it as a running gag.

'No, Jack. Something really sweet.'

'Something really sweet.' And then she laughed her hearty laugh: crazy old Jack.

Sitting on the toilet once, he discovered that she was looking at him through the crack in the door. She'd been standing there for minutes: 'I want to know everything about you.' She looked at his hands and said: 'All those little cells in your skin, those are actually all little Jacks. When I think that, is that love?'

And when Jacques looked in the mirror and saw how ugly he was, with his flabby face, his red, sweaty eyes, his flaky scalp, his beard, then his heart leapt in him, because he knew that her love wasn't prompted by the man he was now, but by the boy from Ostend.

The Ford Falcon survived everything: heat, dust, the most horrible roads, the thump of a kangaroo – which turned out to still be alive, and which Monique put out of its misery with her pistol – loose sand, riverbeds they had to cross. But against pointy stones and round cactuses they could do nothing; the puncture count soon entered the double digits.

One time they got two flat tires at once, on a lonely road through nowhere, at the start of their journey when they still had to discover that two spares was the bare minimum in these parts. They had to wait half the day before a car came by that could call for help, then half the night before the lights of the rescuers popped up: two old men in a pickup with a bed full of Ford Falcon wheels.

Jacques hadn't been scared for a moment. Their spot was wonderfully empty: reddish earth stretching out to the horizon in all directions, with green tufts of grass, low bushes and the road as the only intrusions on the uniformity. Time went by as though it had lumps in it: telling the story of thirty years took five minutes, running your hand through your beard took an hour.

Once the sun had lost its heat, but while it was still light, he agreed to have Monique give him a golf lesson. Her balls soared through the air in graceful arches, causing little eclipses on their way to spots where only generations who no longer knew what golf was would find them. And while a ball he'd hit rose and fell again, and her distant cheer of approval reached his ears, Jacques suddenly saw it. It wasn't him anymore. He was Leslie, his head was bald, he wasn't wearing a single thread that had ever been worn by Jacques Bekker.

Where, then, was Jacques Bekker? He'd committed suicide – and was living life to the hilt!

MONIQUE HAD NOT EXAGGERATED about being famous; she was in the paper and on television every day. A cyclone of curiosity roared around her, and then they would step outside: calm. During the first few days Jacques had felt as if he had a jangling alarm clock at his side, but that feeling made way for exuberant pleasure at their invisibility. People simply didn't see it. It was hilarious: a whole country was dying for a chance to see her, and seeing her they were, but he was the only one who knew what he was seeing: Madame Twenty, eating a sausage on a low wall beside a parking lot; climbing on to the roof of a campground lavatory to fetch their frisbee. It was like being clairvoyant, a clairvoyant who could see into the present.

He didn't know what amazed him more, Monique being Madame Twenty, or her being the girl from Ostend.

Sometimes he thought she could hardly be more than a distant aunt to that girl, an actress who'd once played her. It was strange to read about a Monique who hadn't been bothered by the fact that she existed only in his thoughts; who had done all kinds of things of which he hadn't had the slightest idea, like a child who has promised to stay on the sidewalk but has made a trip to the moon. Monique on a beach in Sydney, wearing the first Madame Twenty bathing suit, Monique receiving a commendation from the Prime Minister, Monique golfing with Crocodile Dundee for a good cause – and, with all of these things, Jacques couldn't help feeling that she should actually have asked him for permission.

She was a grandmother.

He could never have guessed that life, but he had nevertheless already seen the seed of it back in Ostend. She'd been dreaming of the Olympic Games, and that dream had come true, in Tokyo in 1964; the first Belgian springboard diver ever to have made it that far. On both the three- and ten-meter boards she had come in second to last, but she had also met Howard George, an Australian yachtsman fifteen years her senior, heir to a family garment business. She had married him, gone to live in Sydney, was discovered as a TV personality during her very first appearance on a talk show, started her own clothing line within her husband's company, under the name 'Madame Twenty' – and before she turned thirty she had two daughters, her own television show, she'd grown head and shoulders above Howard, divorced him, and then bought him out.

And as Madame Twenty, the provincial Belgian girl Monique Ilegems had become an Australian success story, a household name – famous from panels and talk shows, photos and fashion sections, the clothes she sold, the millions she earned and the flair with which she spent them.

And each time that name, Madame Twenty, awakened something in him, something much deeper than the shop at the airport in Sydney. Monique said she had invented it on the air, during her television debut. That's what the papers said too. First shot, bull's-eye. The way she was.

The pieces Jacques read must have been written as obituaries, but then again, for businesspeople like her, perhaps in anticipation of a fall. One of them – with the headline END OF THE ROAD FOR MADAME TWENTY – he read again and again, because it was also about her younger years in Belgium. At eighteen, during the World's Fair in Brussels, she had worked as an information hostess at the American pavilion. Precisely because he already knew that, he couldn't keep his eyes off the sentence that said it. It was as though the moment in Ostend when she'd told him that herself still lived on in it.

The paper flew out of his hand, Monique had given it a whack.

'End of the road?' she shouted. 'Ha! This is the *beginning* of the road!'

BUT HOW COULD HE, who had simply shown up on her street out of the blue, have become her whole life? What would that life be if he was no longer there?

It was creepy: as though she was skating on ice with no water under it.

AS SOON AS THEY were finished with Australia, they would start on the world. Nothing would get in their way, her money was limitless. Sixty-eight million! To Jacques, the seven hundred thousand she had with her already seemed inexhaustible – how then to comprehend what sixty-eight million dollars meant? A jackpot of one hundred dollars every second for two weeks. A Ford Falcon every day for twenty years. They would be weightless, could go wherever they wanted, to Ecuador and Egypt, Tierra del Fuego and Alaska, Ostend and Amsterdam. In Amsterdam he would go to the archives and read in old newspapers about the mystery he must have become, walk past old haunts in perfect disguise and watch from the far side of the canal as Sonja left her institute. He would follow her, but not when she went into a café. He'd go look at her house too, not in the morning, but during the day, to reduce the risk of seeing her come out the door with a man. And then he'd slide an envelope full of money through her mail slot. No note; she'd know it was from him. How much depended on what he could tuck away without Monique noticing. That wouldn't be any problem, though; she treated her banknotes like they were hand-bills, and, besides, her money was his money; he usually had thousands in his money belt. Ten thousand should be easy enough, maybe even a hundred thousand.

What would Sonja's face look like when she opened that mysterious envelope and found the money? She'd know he wasn't dead, and therefore that he was a bastard who'd kept her worried — but also that he was thinking of her — and that he was sorry.

'A penny for your thoughts,' Monique said.

They were tearing down a red road, away from nothing, toward nothing.

MADAME TWENTY WAS SPOTTED from Perth to Brisbane, from Batemans Bay to Gympie, but no one really believed she was still in Australia. She must have left the country, on the very same day the little neighbor girl had seen her loading suitcases into her car. She was probably sitting high and dry with her millions in Europe, or in South America, along with her equally fugitive 'financial officer and life partner' Alan Wolpe – the man with whom Jacques had heard her make an appointment that first day, the appointment she hadn't kept.

Monique figured Wolpe was angry, and that he'd left Australia. Maybe he was in South Africa, he had friends there. As soon as she was out of the country herself, she'd contact him and give him his due – half of what was in their Swiss bank account.

Jacques saw Wolpe almost every day as well, usually the same five-year-old photos and TV footage: with Monique on the steps of a courthouse, laughing freely after their now clearly undeserved acquittal in the Sea-wear affair. A heavy, square-postured man of fifty-nine with a gravelly face and a moist, obscene gash of a mouth

– he shouldn't go to prison for fraud, but for appearing in public with that mouth uncovered.

Monique's affair with him had lasted ten years – there was no spot on her body where that mouth hadn't been. She must have molded to him like a pen to a hand, and when she caressed Jacques he knew that those caresses had arisen on Wolpe's body.

Whoopie, that was how she pronounced his name.

One evening in their motel room, when Wolpe hadn't even waited for the zapping but showed his mug by the first light of the screen, Jacques could no longer contain himself.

'How could you, with that man!' he exclaimed.

'I *relished* him,' Monique said.

Even after reading the articles she'd recommended, Jacques understood very little – as little as she herself, she claimed – of the Madame Twenty affair. All he knew was that it took place far from the suckers who made the goods and bought them, and that it would cost the Australian government a fortune just to find – amid the labyrinth Wolpe had created and which he knew like the back of his hand – the loopholes through which he'd sluiced away the funds.

'A genius at earning money,' Monique said. 'If only I was half as good at spending it.'

★   ★   ★

SOMETIMES JACQUES THOUGHT ABOUT how strange it was that he had broken off his life for a woman who said 'bingo' instead of 'yes', who'd had her picture taken in a captain's hat amid the glistening beach boys of the surfing team she sponsored, who – listing under the weight of her jewels – launched a new Madame Twenty perfume, owned a corporation on the Cayman Islands, a race-horse. Someone he could never talk to about his blue dreams, who wasn't his type.

But maybe the point wasn't the way things were, but the headline with which you could tell them to yourself: WRITER (47) PAMPERED BY FILTHY RICH CELEBRITY.

Talk always turned to money, and to why a person as rich as her would want to pull the rug out from under half a city, just to steal another couple of million.

'Habit,' she would say.

'You cheated a lot of people.'

'Sure, how else? They received good compensation, they could go straight ahead and build up new, dreary lives. And what if I *did* ruin them? I was in the Olympics. I came in twenty-sixth on the three-meter board and thirty-fourth on the ten. That caused me more pain than I ever caused the entire workforce at Seawear. Were those other girls supposed to fall on their butts in the water to keep me from feeling the pain?'

'That was a fair contest.'

'I had no talent, you call that fair? My talent was to be Madame Twenty, so was I supposed to let everyone else go first again?'

'You had an easy start, with Howard's money.'

'Oh yeah? Didn't I deserve it for being so attractive? He didn't fall in love with just anyone.'

'I think you should give those people at Seawear their money back.'

'If you pay for the helicopter to sprinkle it around.'

'You're a bad person, Monique.'

'That's what I've been trying to tell you all along! I'm a bitch! I invented it. *How to Be a Bitch.* By Madame Twenty. In one long lesson.' And when he remained silent: 'Don't you want to know what that lesson is? Life!'

Her dime-store sarcasm irritated Jacques, but her refusal to simply say what he wanted to hear, or even to toss back the accusation that he seemed to have no trouble helping her spend that money, was something he admired. Could he really find despicable in others what he didn't have, or understand, himself? Maybe owning a racehorse wasn't all that repugnant, maybe it was fun to have a yacht, a private island. And she didn't seem to suffer from not having them anymore. Or were roadside restaurants and a second-hand Ford Falcon actually the romantic clichés of the jet set?

The ironclad good humor with which Monique refused to linger over the ruins of her life Jacques admired as well. All ruined, everything done and gone? – that kind of thing wasn't even part of her vocabulary. With the same courage she'd applied to build it up, she now watched from motel rooms as her life's work crumbled away bit by bit. Garbage bags full of confiscated bookkeeping were dragged out of her main office in Sydney, a subsidiary was sold, production in India halted, bankruptcy filed. She would moan a little, but nothing different from the way she'd moan at the forecast of a rainy day, and with an apologetic little smile for Jacques.

This was one tough lady.

Her house was estimated at three million dollars, and she cheerfully hammered their tent pegs into the ground. She had dined with the fabulously rich and the fabulously famous, and she dove into the greasy potato omelets served them at roadside restaurants. Everywhere they went she could point to billboards for the million-dollar business she had run, and when Jacques said he was thirsty she jumped up and got him a beer. But when they barbecued, *he* had to chop the wood with the special hatchet she'd bought. The woman grills, the man chops.

She wanted to play cards and win, swim and win;

when they visited national parks, she always picked out the longest hike. And when Jacques suggested that eight hours might be a little too far, she replied that 'too far' was the ideal distance for a hike. When there were chasms, she dangled her toes over the edge.

She was a macho.

And when he told her that, she said: 'Yeah, macho girl', and struck a Tarzan pose.

She could be caught, she knew that too. At any moment. But even then: 'It's only our lives, Jack.' Prison was a place you could make the best of too. A matter of A: wanting, and B: doing.

There were predictable moments of suspense: in a movie theater they overheard a conversation about Madame Twenty; Monique was sitting beside the TV screen in a pub full of rednecks when her picture suddenly appeared; a policeman checked her driver's license and missed his shot at national fame. She didn't even blink. At a grocer's store in a country town, with pots of honey so old they should have been taken off the shelf even before Jacques had left for New Zealand, the woman in front of Monique tossed a magazine with Madame Twenty's picture on the cover in with her groceries.

'Oh, *her*,' the shopkeeper growled. 'She's been in

Switzerland for ages. Good on her, far as I'm concerned. Only, she should dump that Wolpe fellow.'

'She'll never do that,' Monique said, and tossed the magazine in with her shopping as well.

HE WAS PART OF her disguise; he came to know a glance with which Monique was sometimes looked at, in which recognition was mingled with disbelief at that recognition – and then, after a glance at him, only the disbelief remained. That wasn't Alan Wolpe . . . so it wasn't her. The cliché protected her as well: anyone who had seen her at Batemans Bay or Gympie simply didn't know how the world was put together; people like Madame Twenty had been in Rio for ages already.

And even if she *was* recognized, which Jacques thought he saw happen on a few occasions, that didn't necessarily have consequences. Madame Twenty was well liked in Australia; the tenor of the news showed sympathy for the collapse of her life's work, almost outright admiration. She'd made it, and now she was making it again by not being caught.

SOMETIMES JACQUES WONDERED WHETHER he shouldn't be doing something else with his life, something other than sitting in a car. And then he believed again that he could ride forever in the Ford Falcon, through red, scorched, endless Australia, with the dream girl of his youth.

But am I really in love with you, granny? he sometimes wondered.

4

THE MEDITERRANEAN WAS too far for the moped after all. They left it in Paris and hitched on, leaving the route to their drivers. For the first time, Jacques was in Switzerland and Italy and on the Côte d'Azur, but Oppy's remained in his thoughts. And when they had a falling out, it was fine by him, because Peter didn't feel like going to Ostend again. Jacques hitchhiked back to Paris alone, picked up his moped and, on a Friday evening three days before school started, he was back in Oppy's, the day's kilometers still buzzing through his body. Beside the little dais with the jukebox, a girl in sunglasses was sitting now – the girl who had been missing the first time. She was with a man, and danced with him every once in a while. Jacques looked at her, and sensed that behind her sunglasses and over the shoulder of that man, she was looking back. She left without him having spoken to her.

So sure he was that he should be at Oppy's that, when he came back the next evening, it was only natural that the girl with the sunglasses was there too, this time with a girlfriend. He asked her to dance. Her cheek came close to his, and she said 'Thank you' when he brought her back to her table. The next time they danced he found out her name was Christa, and that she was the junior gymnastics champion of East Flanders province. She did other sports as well, and she was one of the best trampolinists in Belgium, but there were no official championships for that. She was nineteen, and refused to believe he was sixteen. He kissed her on the cheek, and she kissed him back with a grin. He asked her why she was laughing. 'Because you're sixteen,' she said. The girlfriend disappeared.

Oppy's closed at one, but Christa didn't feel like going home yet. They went to a darker discotheque that stayed open later, and when that one closed as well they went down to the waterfront, where the doorman at an all-night café refused to believe that Jacques was twenty-one. He took her back to her boarding house, and there Christa discovered that she had lost her key. There was nothing to do but wait till morning; it wasn't the kind of place where you could ring the bell at two-thirty.

They wandered around dark Ostend, and sat for a long time on one of the stone stairs from the boulevard to the beach. It was high tide, and the steps led right down into the shiny waves. On those stairs, Christa became the fourth girl with whom Jacques had French-kissed; she held her tongue still in her mouth while he moved his over it.

He put his hand on her breast, and she pulled it away and cried a little. Nothing was said about it, but he knew it was terrible. She had offered him the highest, and he had wanted the lowest. And after they parted at her boarding house at eight, he went back to the camp-ground, took down his tent and drove to Amsterdam with only one thought: he would never forget this night, and in the letters they would write he would show how highly he thought of her.

LATER, WHEN JACQUES RE-READ Christa's letters, he saw that his mysterious woman of Ostend had been an innocent, motherly, provincial girl. She asked him whether he thought it was frivolous of her to like dancing, made him promise to do his homework well, cried over a crippled boy she had met, and forgave him for being in favor of sex before marriage – but then, she forgave him everything. The two of them would just always be the only ones who understood each other.

He himself must have been the most frivolous thing in her life: a schoolboy from Amsterdam with whom she exchanged hot kisses through the mail, while a mining engineer, a man of twenty-eight, had already asked for her hand! She turned him down and the engineer accepted a position in the Congo, and Jacques knew he was the one to blame.

She read novels about life, and passed the titles along to him, the postman fell in love with her, her brother entered the priesthood, she and a girlfriend qualified for the Belgian national gymnastics championship which would also serve as the qualifying round for the Olympic Games. In the train on her way back from a match she had shown Jacques' photo to a couple of girls from her club. 'I should never have done that,' she wrote, 'but I did it anyway. Jacques, tell me truthfully, was that bad of me?'

Their plans to see each other soon didn't work out. She had no free time that her father didn't check up on, and Bijlaar, her village in the countryside between Brussels, Antwerp and Gent, was too far from Amsterdam.

They would have to wait until next summer.

5

THE FORD FALCON was in the Safeway parking lot at Cairns, on the northeast coast of Queensland. Jacques was waiting behind the wheel. He and Monique had done their shopping, and now she'd gone to the launderette. Pickups drove in and out, their beds full of dogs and children, pennants were flapping everywhere, and music blasted from loudspeakers, interrupted occasionally by a man on a podium who shouted to come up and try the latest fruit juice.

In a little less than two weeks, their plane would leave Darwin for London, and having the tickets gave Jacques a constant sense of excitement. But now he let his newspaper settle on to the steering wheel and stared ahead, at a little cluster of phone booths at the edge of the parking lot. It had happened, the thing that had to happen sometime and that he had secretly longed for, but which, now that it *had* happened, left a heaviness in his chest. On one of the inside pages was a picture of himself: DUTCH TV HOST DISAPPEARS DURING SYDNEY STOPOVER – LAST SEEN ON CIRCULAR QUAY.

It took a moment before he could place the photo: Edith had taken it in Sydney, on Circular Quay, at the moment of his disappearance. Anna must have been in the picture too, but she had been cut out.

Marjike Eerhard, the official chaperone of the cultural mission to New Zealand in which Bekker (47) had taken part, had stayed behind in Sydney for two days to look for him, then returned to the Netherlands empty-handed. Nothing had been heard from him since; an accident or foul play seemed likely. According to the two traveling companions who had seen him last, Bekker had said he had 'a demon to drive out in Sydney'. That meant he had had a plan; anyone knowing what that was, was urged to report. An investigation in the Netherlands had uncovered no leads.

Marj*i*ke: those two letters transposed in her name were like a slip that was showing, a crookedly buttoned blouse; a humiliation she suffered because of him. And it was as if through that, and through Anna's being cut out of the photo, he realized what a bastard he was, and how much he missed everything.

He could see his house, clocks ticking away there, his answering machine perhaps still gathering messages, but then: who would still call him? They all knew he didn't exist anymore. The police would have been to his house by now, maybe *they* had found Monique's address amid his jumble. If so, the case was solved: people who keep each other's addresses don't accidentally disappear on the same day. He would be unmasked before the eyes of Holland: no hero taken tragically by some mysterious calamity, but a man who had let his friends worry themselves to death so he could run off with a woman.

He wasn't *that* much of a bastard. But that much of a bastard was how he felt.

But what else could he have done?

Monique would have lived on in him for thirty years in vain if he hadn't gone with her once he had the chance. But she was not his girlfriend; he couldn't see the two of them as a couple. She was something from beyond reality, and to be with her anyway he'd had to disappear along with her into their own private bubble in reality. That bubble would burst as soon as he was connected to something real, something as actual as Sonja, and that was why he hadn't called her.

From between the parked cars, Monique suddenly appeared: a cheerful, spectacled woman in ridiculous red shorts, toting a heavy bag full of laundry. Jacques jumped out of the car to help, but she made him sit down again, and close his eyes. She had a surprise.

73

Beside him on the front seat he heard the crackle of paper, the peep of Styrofoam, the clatter of little glass plates.

Then there was a click, the sound of Monique giggling in anticipation, and something was pushed into Jacques' ear. A vision arose, at the same moment it came true: the Saskatchewan Club, Sunday afternoon, the last dance before her train left. Violins whined, and Brenda Lee sang 'I'm Sorry'.

He opened his eyes. Monique was looking straight at him. Between them lay a portable CD player, with at least ten CDs, all music from back then.

'I really am sorry,' she said. 'It's always been on my mind.'

'What was the joke?' he asked. 'The joke in your note?'

'Nothing. There wasn't any joke. It was impossible, so then it's better to rip the Band-Aid off in one go.'

He listened on, but Ostend had disappeared from the song; he'd heard it too often. When it was finished, he pulled out the earplug and handed her the newspaper.

'So,' she said after she finished the article, 'you were going to drive out a demon. And? Did you manage?'

And suddenly he knew the chance had already come and gone: the chance to love her – that the demon *had* been driven out, that the promise of Oppy's had been

this, their ramble through Australia, and that now he
could go home.

'No,' he said.

'Well, you won't either, Jack.'

WHAT HE HAD OVERLOOKED, Monique saw immediately:
the newspaper article meant the end of the Ford Falcon.
Jacques' photo was probably in papers all over Australia,
and would be broadcast on TV as well. And even if he
didn't look the way he had when he bought the Ford
Falcon – if the used-car dealer recognized his photo their
invisibility would be lifted; they could be recognized
anywhere, simply by their license plate.

For ten thousand dollars, Monique bought a white
Ford Fairmont, and when darkness came they transferred
their baggage at a deserted parking lot along the beach.
And just like long ago on Eurella Street, they left the
keys in the car, hoping that a finder would move their
tracks. Only after driving a hundred kilometers south did
they stop at a motel.

The Fairmont was prettier, cleaner and more power-
ful, it hugged the road better, and it made clear that the
Ford Falcon had been the soul of their adventure.

THE PHONE RANG. Sonja, Jacques thought, but Monique
answered it.

It was dark. He remembered that they were in a hotel in Alice Springs, that his plane would be leaving for Europe in three days, and fell asleep again.

When Monique woke him, he saw on the clock radio that it was a little past five. She was already dressed, in clothes he had never seen before: a long blue dress with thin shoulder straps, a necklace, earrings, high heels – evening wear.

She made him get up too, put on clothes that were lying ready for him. He didn't understand what was going on, and only in front of the mirror did he discover that he was wearing a white tuxedo. Rage welled up in him: what did she think he was? Some kind of monkey? Where did she come up with this nonsense? And what was this masquerade party all about, in the middle of the night?

She held him at arm's length and nodded approvingly: it fit.

'Happy birthday,' she said.

In the course of their journey Jacques had lost track of everything that was normal, and he was still half asleep, but he was sure it was nowhere near his birthday. Even so, it *was* his birthday: Leslie Elder's birthday. He was turning fifty, and this was the surprise with which they were going to celebrate it.

There was a knock at the door, and a few moments

later they were sitting in a van, moving down the darkened lanes of Alice Springs. In open countryside they stopped beside another van with a trailer. Men in overalls were walking around, and on the ground was a huge, dark shape that moved lightly, as if breathing, and slowly grew bigger. It was a balloon filling with hot air: the burners' flaming blasts sounded like sheets being torn to shreds.

Monique had hired a balloon for him, for his birthday.

Far away the darkness was fading, the first announcement of daylight. A fresh, lovely heat brushed Jacques' cheeks. The men shouted directions to each other, their voices clear as blades on the bottom of a mountain stream. Slowly the balloon rose up, like the inquisitive, floundering erection of some giant beast, until it finally stood upright, swaying lightly in the gentle breeze.

They climbed into the basket, the ropes were thrown loose, and they rose, silently and evenly. The crew consisted of a man and a boy, Wayne and Peter, in red overalls with 'Outback Ballooning' emblems. Occasionally, when Wayne told him to, Peter pulled on a handle and a burst of flame shot up, and Jacques felt the heat briefly, like sitting beside a fireplace.

They leaned over the edge of the basket, their arms around each other. The sun came up, and behind them appeared their shadow; a balloon tall as a church. Hordes of kangaroos, big and small, skipped along with them soundlessly, at exactly the same speed, as though they'd been hired to do so and might go about their own business in a minute. Every once in a while, along the little roads or in the wild countryside below, they could see the two vans trying to follow them, stopping sometimes while they figured out which road to take. Jacques sensed that Wayne was keeping radio contact to a minimum, in order not to break the silence.

There was no rocking, almost no wind. The sun climbed, the endless landscape had a clarity that almost made you blush. Jacques felt completely free, like on those days back when summer vacation had already begun and you were still at home, and went swimming or sailing. Only three more days! He was almost there, the most amazing adventure of his life was finished, the detour completed. It was even as if he had fallen in love – but then maybe you always fell in love with the person with whom you shared relief, even if that relief was at being freed from her.

'It's a dream,' he said.

'Yes,' Monique said. 'And when we wake up from that dream, let it be in each other's arms.'

He shivered, and at the same time he thought her reply was beautiful, and wished he had thought of it himself. Fear seized him, the fear that now there was nothing else he could think of but to be happy.

It was still before eight, but already hot, when they landed at an open spot among low trees. Jacques knew what was coming: a champagne breakfast in the desert; he had seen the folders lying around back at the hotel. It was horribly pathetic to think that something like this was worth doing, but at the same time it was the sweetest birthday surprise anyone had ever given him. Within a few minutes the vans arrived, the balloon was folded up and put in the basket on the trailer, and Jacques and Monique were sitting beneath parasols at a long table in the middle of the clearing, drinking champagne.

She gave him a gold fountain pen. On it was engraved: *For Leslie, from Paula*.

They were left in peace, occasionally someone came by to pour some champagne or bring them more oysters or smoked salmon. No one stared at them, the waiters kept their distance, their backs turned to them. Jacques was sure the entire crew knew who Monique was, but it was as though it didn't matter, as though they were an empress and an emperor who had come to this remote place for a ceremony, and for whom everything possible would be done to make them feel they were alone.

Jacques got drunk, what else could he do?

'You won't just up and leave me, will you, Jack?'

Monique said, and a cold fear that she knew everything rushed through his veins.

'No – no.'

'Say something sweet to me.'

He looked at her. What was he doing with this dolled-up, lonely, hopelessly happy lady with her pitiful balloon trip?

'I love you,' he said.

6

THIS TIME JACQUES went alone, and Ostend was his
destination. While he waited for Christa, who – at
the last moment – wasn't coming for a whole week as
planned but only for a weekend, he spent his time at
Oppy's, adding to the list of girls he'd kissed.

The letters she sent to the campground were increas-
ingly desperate. The gymnastics had taken up so much
time; her father didn't want her spending even more
time on a trip to the coast; the weekend became a day,
and was finally called off altogether. Under no circum-
stances was he to come to Bijlaar. The only chance they
had to see each other was on a Sunday afternoon, in
Brussels.

He hitchhiked there, it was a gray day. On a little
square in front of the station he waited, afraid he
wouldn't recognize her. The girl who walked out of
the station entrance at the appointed hour, who couldn't

possibly *not* be Christa, was uglier than he had feared, with wispy hair and spectacles; the sunglasses of Ostend had been camouflage. Despite all the kisses in their letters, it was suddenly unclear how they were to greet each other, and Jacques' mouth ended up against her collar.

He had been wondering what they were going to do, but Christa had the day all mapped out in her mind – their last. After today they wouldn't see each other anymore, and there would be no more letters. 'A death sentence,' Jacques said, on the rear platform of the tram. She took him to the house of an aunt, who was gone that afternoon, to a sofa that was there, and there they lay for their final hours together, pressed tightly against each other.

'Oh Jacques,' she sighed, 'I pray that no bad woman will ever come into your life.'

Jacques realized that, ever since they'd met, it had been certain that their reunion would also be their parting for all time: what else could there be after the fulfillment of a dream, except emptiness? But now they were still in each other's arms. The following moment that would still be so, and the moment after that too. Even the very last minute on the sofa would have a beginning, a middle, and only then an end. And after that there would be the walk to the tram, the tram ride back to the station. But still, suddenly, there he was, and her train was gone.

THAT CHRISTA'S DISAPPEARANCE HAD no effect on the fun at Oppy's did not come as a shock to Jacques. During their year of letter-writing, he'd had a girl in Amsterdam as well; Christa was too elevated to be threatened by everyday matters. He added a Jeanne, an Angela and a Nicole to his list, but one evening he stopped dead in his tracks: at the edge of the dance floor stood the prettiest girl he had ever seen. Boyishly short blonde hair, a festive, tight little figure, nice clothes, a bold glance. And she seemed to be looking at him – smiling at him. He asked her to dance, and when it was over she asked: 'Your name is Jack, isn't it?'

He was stunned. 'Almost right,' he said, 'my name's Jacques. Who told you that?'

'No one. You just look like a Jack, that's all.'

7

J ACQUES LOCKED THE Fairmont and headed back to the
departure hall. An overwhelming feeling of freedom
washed over him. In two hours they'd be sitting in the
plane to London. Or in a jail cell in Darwin, but he
couldn't worry much about the passport control; there
was a later moment that demanded all his worrying: the
moment when he would tell Monique that he wasn't
going any further with her. Where would he do that? In
London, right away? In Zurich, once she had her
money? Or would he stay with her a little longer, just
to taste something of the madness of her millions?

Instead of going into Darwin, they had driven straight
to the airport from Goodilla, a hundred kilometers to the
south along the big road. Last hotel, last night in
Australia, last kangaroo: he was going home. This stroll
to the departure hall was the last part of it.

When he saw a telephone booth, he went into it. He

tossed a dollar in the slot and, his heart pounding like an engine room, he dialed Sonja's number. After the first ring he hung up. A sound that had been produced in Holland! Or did those tones come from a switchboard somewhere in Australia, or even from inside the telephone itself? It didn't matter – that tone was the toast to their speedy reunion.

No: he had to make decisions. No more profiteering. He would say it in London, at the airport. And then he'd fly straight on to Amsterdam, despite the wave of publicity that would crash down on him there, and no pleasant one at that. But he couldn't deny that he was also looking forward to the sensation his disappearance must have caused.

Suddenly he saw Monique. She was standing on the curb in front of the departure hall, her arm raised strangely, a newspaper in her hand. For a moment he was afraid she'd seen him coming out of the phone booth, but from her face, her whole bearing, he could tell that she had just run outside.

On the front page was a photo of Wolpe. In big, fat, black letters above it, it said: ALAN WOLPE DEAD IN DARWIN CELL.

AT THE MOMENT THEIR plane took off, they were racing past the motel in Goodilla. Monique drove south blindly, without asking him to take the wheel, not on her way to any place but to a time: six p.m. – nine o'clock in the morning Swiss time.

Wolpe had committed suicide. He had arrived in Darwin from London the previous afternoon, with a moustache and dyed hair, using the papers of Alan Merribone – *Wolpe* was the one who'd thought Darwin would be safer than Sydney. But they had recognized him, and his passport had proven false. A hundred thousand dollars had been found in his luggage, and during the first round of interrogation he had admitted to being Wolpe. At eight o'clock they'd locked him up, pending the hearing to fix his bail, and at twelve he'd been found dead in his cell. He had probably swallowed a cyanide capsule they had overlooked when they searched him.

Monique had insisted on leaving right away. Wolpe and she, and Jacques as well, had obtained their false passports through the same channels; maybe something had gone wrong there. Customs in Darwin were apparently tipped off, and might be on the lookout now. What's more, Wolpe knew the name Paula Fuerst; he might have given that away.

But there was one word in the article around which everything revolved: Switzerland. If they were right, and Wolpe had really been there, then Monique knew where: in Zurich, on Bahnhofstrasse, in the building of the Union Banquaire Suisse, second floor, the office of Herr Knie. And if that was right, then perhaps it was no use going there anymore. But Knie was still asleep, and they were speeding into Australia again, waiting until he arrived at his office.

AT SIX THEY STOPPED in Larrimah: a couple of houses, a gas station and a phone booth. Jacques made the call; Monique was afraid her voice would be recognized at a switchboard somewhere. The Union Banquaire Suisse came across clear as crystal: it was Friday, Knie's day off. He would be back again on Monday. Monique swore – and on they drove, deeper into the country. Jacques was crushed. He'd been so close! And now he had to go along again, into Australia. In Darwin he should have told her it was over, asked her for his ticket, or bought one for himself if she didn't want to give it to him. But he had been afraid of her rage and her misery. And now he felt like he was made of lead, partly because they had been close to that fat, dead body and because Wolpe, like him, had been a participant in Monique's adventure and had paid for that with his life.

The horror, the incomprehensibility of suicide! Suddenly realizing that it was true, that you were going to do it, that everything was over. What would it feel like to know that you had one hour, one minute left to live? Were you frightened, or perhaps exuberant, like at the start of a vacation? Old Wolpe had been pretty fearless! If it was true about that suicide capsule, then his trip to Darwin had been a life-or-death gamble. He boards the plane: he's alive. He lands: he's alive. He goes into the passport area, and he's still alive. Someone says: 'Would you please come with me?' – and he knows he's dead.

After his arrest he had lived on for eight hours with that pill in his pocket, or somewhere far up his ass. The last four hours he'd spent in a cell. They had checked on him there every fifteen minutes; at a quarter to twelve he had still been sitting on his cot, reading. And then he'd done it.

An opened roll of peppermints had been found on the cot in his cell. Had he put one in his mouth and thought: 'This is my last peppermint'? How did that go, did you pick a moment, did you suddenly muster up the courage? Did you notice – wondering when you would do it, or whether you would do it at all – that you had suddenly *already* done it, the way, in bed in the morning and thinking about getting up, you always realized that you *had* already gotten up?

Wolpe had three children and a grandchild, a little girl who would turn six two days from now. He was a skydiver, and he had lost a toe in a nasty fall he'd taken once while water-skiing, dressed as Santa Claus for his children.

Why hadn't Monique told him things like that? Or hadn't she known herself, was she reading it now for the first time in the newspaper?

By Monday evening they were in Marree, a former camel driver's station at the junction of two desert routes, the Oodnadatta Track and the Birdsville Track, twenty-six hundred kilometers from Darwin. They found a hotel and at six o'clock they walked to a phone booth, beside a vacant lot where a camel was kneeling on the ground; a sign there said you could ride on its back for ten dollars. Across the road was a pub, the Oodnadatta Inn; before the entrance, a boy with a garden hose was spraying the road to keep too much dust from blowing in.

Jacques went into the booth and, standing with his back to Monique, dialed the number of the bank. He was put through in the same breath.

'Knie,' said the other side of the world.

'My name is Oldfield,' Jacques said, 'and I would like some information about an account.'

'That's possible. But then you'll have to come to our offices.'

'That's a twenty-four-hour flight for me.'

'I'm afraid there's nothing I can do about that.'

'I'm calling on behalf of someone who has an account with your bank. Number 36EA38Q3.' He repeated it slowly, and thought he heard the rattle of a keyboard.

'I can't give you any information about that account, Mr Oldfield.'

'I was told that the number would be enough to get information.'

'That's correct, in principle.'

'So why can't you give me any information?'

'The account you mentioned has been terminated.'

'Terminated? What does that mean?'

'There is no account number 36EA38Q3.'

'But there was at one time?'

The silence, which lasted a few seconds each time because the words had to travel halfway around the world, was longer now.

'Yes,' Knie said.

'So the person who had that account no longer has any money in your bank?'

'No.'

'Has a Mr Wolpe been to see you?'

'If I knew a Mr Wolpe, I wouldn't tell you,' Knie said. Only now did it occur to Jacques that Knie, in his office in Zurich, knew – and was probably seeing on the screen right in front of him – exactly what this call meant:

Monica George had finally discovered that her co-signer had doublecrossed her, and that she had lost her millions.

Jacques thanked him, hung up and left the phone booth.

Monique was leaning against a fence post.

'He emptied the account,' he said.

She nodded briefly, deep in thought, then crossed the road to the boy with the hose and held up her hands for water. She splashed her face and the back of her neck, gave the boy a dollar and shouted: 'Champagne!'

THEIR ENTRANCE AT THE Oodnadatta Inn knocked a hole in a roar of sound – then everyone went on shouting. The men had bare arms and wore hats, almost all of them had beards, the women had red hair, and everyone had a can of beer. In a corner, darts were thumping into cork. The back wall of the bar was a collage of banknotes from all over the world; there was an old Dutch five-guilder bill, but Jacques couldn't locate a single Belgian one.

'Somethin' to celebrate?' said the man behind the bar when Monique ordered champagne.

'The end of my worries.'

Ordering champagne in a bar like this was asking for attention, and Jacques felt and saw eyes turn on her. She saw it too, but she didn't seem to care anymore. What was this champagne all about? About acting tough despite all the money she had lost, but also because she knew the moment had come: End of the Road for Madame Twenty. Her money was gone, she sensed he wanted out. She couldn't keep running forever. What else could she do, once the bottle was empty, but ask for the nearest police station and turn herself in? Tomorrow, around their hotel, the phone booth, the boy with the garden hose, camera crews from all over Australia would be jostling for a shot. And here: the people who were seeing them now would tell what they were seeing – if he scratched his head, they would say: he scratched his head. Their invisibility had changed into the opposite; it was as though all of Australia was already looking at them through the eyes of these drinkers.

The television behind the bar was on, and suddenly a face appeared on the screen that made Jacques' flesh creep: a creased, spectacled caricature of a face. He had no idea who it was, or even if it was a man or a woman, but he still seemed to know that face. In fact, it was also the words BELGIAN TV at the bottom of the screen that startled him. BELGIAN TV: with Wolpe dead, it had to be about Monique. The absurd gray pompadour, like some cartoon character's, finally made him see that this was a woman in her fifties. She seemed on the verge of tears, but the sound was down too low to hear what she was saying.

Monique watched too, her mouth open.

The woman disappeared, but she'd be back – it was only a preview from news that was about to begin.

'Do you recognize her?' Monique asked.

'No.'

'She's the joke.'

It was Christa. How cruel time had been to her! It almost made him cry himself, but he walked up to the bar and asked them to turn up the sound. It violated all their safety measures, but Christa's appearance seemed to relieve him of all obligations.

She was back.

She knew Madame Twenty, she knew Jacques Bekker, and she knew that they knew each other. She had brought them together, without meaning to. The two disappearances were one.

Monique, she explained in the unaffected voice of an Australian anchorwoman, had been her best friend, Jacques a Dutch boy who had been her pen-pal. And with whom she had been in love. Monique had said she was going to steal him from her. At first it had seemed like a joke, but she had done it, and to prove it she had shown everyone a photo of her with Jacques.

It was enough to bring tears of laughter to your eyes, this ghastly provincial schoolmarm who could barely control her own tears as she told some thirty-year-old

93

love story, and who had been the rival of a flamboyant celebrity like Madame Twenty!

'What did she have to be jealous of?' the invisible Australian woman said. 'She was pretty, I was ugly. The boys looked at her, not at me. So why did she have to steal Jacques from me?'

Christa disappeared. A yacht had run onto the rocks near Fremantle.

Jacques sensed that he was no longer alone in front of the TV: Monique was standing beside him. Gradually he realized how quiet the Oodnadatta Inn had become. Eyes turned away when he looked. So this was the way it went, being recognized. Monique laid her hand on his arm, but he shook it off. He walked outside.

THE BLAZING SUN MADE a pile driver go up and down in his head. He walked past the telephone booth, the camel was still there. Young Aborigines were cutting figures on racing bikes in a parking lot. The streets were deserted. It was as if all of Ostend disappeared into an abyss. It had been a betrayal, a frame-up, a nasty trick on a girlfriend. She had come to Ostend as a *joke*, she had known that she'd find him there, and that she would ditch him immediately – off to the next lark! It had all been a sham, up to and including the taxi she'd made him take to Leichhardt Street.

How could he have been so blind?! Two girls, both gymnasts, the same age, both in Ostend, both at Oppy's. Monique had even known his name, and he had believed her when she said she had guessed it. He was disgusted by his own gullibility, his inability to see that people could be so cunning. And yet: that morning in his tent. She had already taken what she wanted, so why had there been that morning?

He laughed and shook his head – she had still needed the photo.

He turned a corner and saw her.

He wanted to slip away, not be seen by her now that he was so betrayed, but he stopped, and she walked up to him.

'I want to go home,' he said. 'I want you to take me to an airport.'

'Okay.'

'Why didn't you ever tell me this?'

'I was afraid.'

'It was a trick on Christa. You only came for a photo. It was all a lie. You no-good, no-good bitch.'

'Come on, Jack. You have to meet somehow, right? What's the lie? That I've been with you for two months now? That I've lost my money because I wanted to go with you, rather than with Alan? Come on, let's go. I need to think. But not here.'

★   ★   ★

WHAT COULD BE LOVELIER than to sit at sunset, with silent pelicans as your only witnesses, drinking champagne on the banks of Lake Eyre, filled with water for the first time in twenty years, when you're down to your last seven hundred and forty thousand dollars?

There was absolutely nowhere they could go.

They had driven back north from Marree, and at the top of a rise they had seen the deep-blue, endless surface of water. That was where Monique wanted to spend the night; there was no place for them anymore in the civilized world. The cutoff to the lake had soon become a faint path, turning into tire tracks after a few minutes, which then disappeared. First across open country, then along the edge of the lake, they had driven on until the wheels of the Fairmont began to sink too far into the saline crust.

The sun was low, the moon had already come up. The light-gray rind and the blue stripe of water lay in an unbelievably clear white light. Big birds flew over the water without breaking the silence, pelicans. Far away they settled down and rose up again; there was a big flock of them out there.

Monique took the cooler and the folding table out of the car and filled their glasses. Then they undressed and walked to the water, quickly sinking to their ankles in the salty crust; at every step there was an anxious moment before you were stopped by a second, harder layer. Black muck gushed up between Jacques' toes. The headache was gone, faded into the tipsiness of champagne.

They had hoped to swim, but no matter how far they walked, the water never came up past their calves. Lake Eyre was bigger than Holland and Belgium put together, but you could probably walk across it without getting your knees wet.

Monique dropped down into the water anyway, and Jacques laid himself down beside her, their backs above the surface.

'Jack, don't leave me alone,' she said.

She put her arms around him, and he put his arms around her. They rolled back and forth a bit in the mud, rocking each other like babies. Her pitifulness was too grotesque for him to be angry with her. She was like a warrior, at once brave and preposterous, who has a spear sticking right through him but goes on fighting. Once she'd gotten over the shock of losing her money, she would go to the police; until then he would stay with her. He had cost her millions; maybe now she had paid for the things she had done. And maybe he understood. Even back then she must have looked at Christa's drab, provincial face and vowed to sidestep that future. He could appreciate that, actually admire her strength in doing it, mean as it was, even though he himself had been the dupe.

The mud stuck black and shiny to their bodies as they walked back. You couldn't rub it off; they'd have to go back to the water with bottles and a sponge, and give each other a shower. The salty crust had bulged up around the footsteps they had left on the way out, like a row of big white slippers they'd lost. There was a slight wind. The Australian night sky was fat with stars. Knie was at his desk.

When they got to the car they heard a growling, so far away that it took a few minutes before they could see where it came from. Along the edge of the lake, almost too small to pick out, a car was coming. In the setting sun it swerved and swayed toward them like a burning boat on a rough sea. Police, Jacques thought. A bad time to be naked; now they had to pull on their clothes over the barely dried crusts of mud. Jacques took a swig from Monique's glass, which was still half full on the folding table; the champagne was lukewarm and sticky, awful.

The intruder turned out to be a grayish-green jeep, battered and raggedy like a stray cat that has had to fight too often. It pulled up beside the Fairmont. Two people got out, a man in his forties and a boy. The music they had on kept playing after the engine was turned off. The man wore glasses with round, rimless lenses.

'Hi,' Jacques said. He stuck up his hand.

The boy remained leaning against the fender, barely looking at them. The man took a few steps forward. 'Hi,' he said. He had a rifle in his hand, a faded purple undershirt with spots on it, bare arms. His hair was thin, a downy gray, and he had a close-cut gray beard. The glasses gave him a surprised, owlish look.

To his horror, Jacques recognized him, and the boy too — from the pub in Marree. He remembered a moment of amazement that, so far out in the bush, one would see a face, the man's, with such fine lines and a certain intelligent sensitivity.

Without actually pointing it at them, the man raised his rifle a little, as though showing a permit.

'We want your money,' he said, 'let's do this fast.' His voice sounded refined. He had a dangerously uncertain gleam in his eye. Jacques' knees were knocking.

'What money?' Monique said. 'Piss off, we don't have any money.'

'You buy things. That money.'

'It's not worth the risk you're taking.'

The man pointed his gun at Monique. 'Come on. Hurry up. Quick. I want to do this fast.' The gun didn't fit him well. 'I want to do this fast,' he repeated. Jacques was paralyzed with fear, and yet completely lucid, as though the four of them in the white moonlight at the edge of Lake Eyre were fish he was looking at in some aquarium. He wondered where he'd seen the man's look before, then remembered: in a porno film. An actress had worn this same look: defiant, and at the same time resigned to the ineradicable shame.

The man licked his lips.

The boy came and stood beside him. 'We don't have any money,' he said, mimicking Monique with a drawl. He nodded his head to the rhythm of the music.

The mud itched under Jacques' clothes. The boy looked a lot like the man. And suddenly he saw it: they were father and son.

'Just give it to them, Leslie,' Monique said. 'The black backpack.' She tossed their money belts to the boy.

Jacques looked at the man. When he nodded, Jacques bent down, picked up the backpack that was leaning against a leg of the folding table and put it on the table. It dawned on him that it was awfully shoddy of them to let him do that himself, and, as though that thought was a portent, he opened the pack and saw Monique's pistol. His heart pounded against his ribs. He didn't know anything about that pistol – did it have a safety catch? And the firm voice in which Monique had commanded him to pick up her backpack – did she expect him to play the hero? To save *her* money? If he grabbed the pistol, havoc would break out here – and no one could tell how much life would be left afterwards. Afraid to even touch the pistol, he reached past it, and at the bottom found the folder containing a few thousand dollars they had put aside for just such an event. He held it up to the boy, who yanked it out of his hand as though he was required to show contempt in everything he did. He started counting right away, his lips moving.

'How much?' the man said.

'Don't know,' the boy said. 'Five or six thousand.'

'You have more than that,' the man said. He was addressing Monique.

'Five thousand seems like plenty to me.'

'Not for Madame Twenty. You're Madame Twenty.'

'People say that all the time. You think Madame Twenty would go to some hole where mugs like you hang out? She's already high and dry in Rio. Fuck off, do you have any idea what five thousand dollars means to us?'

'Yes, nothing.'

'And he's the Dutch quizmaster,' the boy said. He began emptying the Fairmont. He threw everything out: dirty underpants, road maps, bags, candy, golf balls.

'I saw you on the telly,' the man said to Monique. 'Twenty years ago. *Questionable Answers*. You were good, the others were cows.'

Suddenly Jacques knew for sure that this was their first robbery. It must have occurred to them in the pub, and from now on they would always be thugs: this was their initiation. And the boy was the criminal. Maybe the father had come up with the idea, and the boy may have thought he was being dragged along – but this was how the man tried to win his son's approval, the way he may once have broken speed limits for him. His courage was his obligation to display no weakness. And even if he was the sensitive one of the two, that also made him the most dangerous: in order not to lose face, he would stop at nothing.

The boy upended a gym bag: dirty laundry, towels, bundles and loose hundred-dollar bills fell to the ground. He didn't see them until he was already busy shaking out the next bag. A sigh of awe escaped him, and he squatted down beside the money and began scraping it together. Jacques was impressed as well, now that he saw it all spread out for the first time.

'How much is it?' the man asked.

The boy tried to count, but couldn't, there were too many bills, and he was too nervous.

'A hundred and twenty thousand,' Monique said.

The boy stuffed the money back in the bag and brought it to his father.

And now the painless explosion, the void.

But the man said something and the boy popped the hood of the Fairmont, began yanking out wires and hoses and poured two jerrycans of gasoline onto the ground.

The relief made Jacques' head spin: this was their safety measure! They were going to stay alive!

The boy kicked the side of the car, climbed in and began trying to break off the handle of the automatic transmission, tear out the upholstery, threw candy and playing cards on the ground, bent a golf club over the roof.

'The axe,' the man said, nodding at the barbecue hatchet that had fallen to the ground with all the rest. The boy picked it up and began hacking away at the engine block with metallic, thunking sounds. He smashed the windows and kept hacking away until the hatchet lodged in a door panel.

'They've got more,' he said.

For a moment, the man seemed unsure what to do. 'Yes, you have more,' he said. 'He's going to keep looking. If you don't tell us and he finds something, you're dead.'

'The butter dish,' Jacques said. 'In the cooler.'

★   ★   ★

103

THE SUN WAS GONE. There was no bird that flew, only stars and the moon, whitish and so close that it looked like an insanely huge streetlight on an invisible lamppost.

They stood beside each other at the folding table, in the same position in which they'd watched the lights of the robbers' jeep disappear. Monique put her arm around his waist, he put his arm around her shoulder. The mud had dried to a solid crust. Through it he felt her warmth, like that of a child feverish after an exciting parade.

'That moon!' she said. 'Jack, look! Have you ever seen a moon like that?'

Her shoulders began shaking, and he wept along with her, but when he noticed it was laughter it turned out he was laughing too.

'We've got nothing left!' Monique shouted.

'Absolutely nothing!' Jacques shouted.

'All gone, in one day!' she screamed.

They laughed like idiots, and laughed again and again; roaring with laughter, they rolled over the ground, they threw clothes and towels in the air, screamed till their voices were gone, and it felt like a flaw in something perfect when Jacques realized that, somewhere amid the ravage, there had to be a pair of trousers with the money left over from buying the Ford Falcon. He had never laughed like this before, they had already been laughing for longer than the robbery had taken.

To have nothing left, really, absolutely nothing! In this place, with only a moon!

8

H ER NAME WAS Monique Ilegems, and that same
evening she took him to bed.

She was twenty, a dream girl, but the real dream was
how naturally she sat at *his* table, folding paper frogs
that jumped effortlessly over his glass of beer, and
sometimes into it. She had arrived that afternoon on
the train, and had to be home the next morning, but it
was like he was the only thing in Ostend that mattered.
They danced, she nestled her head on his shoulder,
laughed at what he said, and embraced him in their
dark corner at Oppy's. She had her own name for him,
Jack, American-style. She spoke English half the time
anyway: America was her dream and her future. Now
she was still a typist at an American ad agency in
Brussels, but within three years she would be living
there − if he didn't believe it, she would send him a
postcard.

'You can also just tell me,' Jacques said. 'Because I'll be living there with you.'

'You're a crazy boy, Jack,' she said, laughing, and she gave him a kiss.

He should also be aware of the fact that he was sitting at the same table with an Olympic champion: diving, Tokyo 1964. Those Games wouldn't be for another four years; exactly enough time for her to become gold-medal material.

It was almost spooky, the way they understood each other, especially the way she understood him. Her knowing his name must have been a joke, she must have heard someone greet him, but she had also guessed that he wanted to be a writer, that his parents were divorced, that he was the goalie of his soccer team. She asked whether he had ever known a Belgian girl before, and Jacques felt at home enough with her to tell her all about Christa. Really, this Monique was a great girl – and for the first time he wondered whether he might have been mistaken, and the promise of Oppy's had actually been something other than Christa.

WHEN OPPY'S CLOSED, Monique didn't want to go to another discotheque. She climbed on the back of his moped and he brought her to her hotel, far from the center of town on a dark, cobblestone street at the bottom of the sea dike, close to his campground. It was a lonesome white house he must have driven by many times without noticing; and when he discovered, years later, that it had been torn down, he was submerged for days in a mourning that would not go away.

'Thank you for the most magnificent evening of my life,' Jacques said in English. 'Maybe tomorrow I can take you to . . .'

'Come with me,' she said.

She pointed to her window: he was to park his moped somewhere else, wait ten minutes, then come up the fire escape. She would open her window – and that was what this idiot of a memory of his would preserve of his First Time: the fire escape groaning softly in the wind, the clattering of a rope against a flagpole along the boulevard, the lights of ships at sea, a girl going into a hotel, a darkened window behind which she undresses, thinking of you.

9

Dear Sonja,

By the time you read this, I'll be dead. I hear you laugh: oh, Jacques, you're such a ham. But that's the laugh you laugh now, as you read over my shoulder, your ear brushing mine. I'm laughing too, at how interesting I've become now that I'm staring death in the eye.

Monica – the woman for whom I dumped you – and I have been stuck for three days with a wrecked car in the middle of nowhere. It's empty here and indescribably beautiful, and the closest settlement, a place called William Creek, is a hundred kilometers away. We're going to take everything we can of what we have left to eat and drink, and in one hour, when the sun becomes bearable, we'll try to reach William Creek on foot. It's going to be the sort of journey for which you used to get whole deserts named after you, especially if you died in the process. Bekker's Stony Desert: sounds good, doesn't it? We don't have a chance in hell, but it's bound to turn out fine: ending up like a dried-out kangaroo carcass along the Oodnadatta Track, that's not something that happens to quizmasters.

It's enough to make you die laughing: everyone in Australia is looking for us, and we want to be found, but we've given up all hope of that. The first two days we walked out to the road. That alone took us two hours; we drove a lot further into the wilderness than we thought. And than was advisable. And the whole Oodnadatta Track is no more than a bulldozer trail through the void. Nothing ever comes by. The first day we saw a cloud of dust, far away, maybe a car. It took forever before we knew for sure that it was moving *away* from us. We didn't stay there long, it was the middle of the day. You can't imagine this heat; when you see a bird, you hope it will fly over and cast its shadow on you.

On the way back I fell. Suddenly I was lying there, I don't know why. Maybe I was drunk; we drank all our beer first, the soft drinks and water are for later.

Yesterday we went later in the day, and we didn't see a single cloud of dust.

Today we stayed here, the walk to the road takes too much energy in return for too little hope. A plane came by, very far away. We waved and shouted like castaways on a desert island, but it flew on. Maybe it saw that we were here, but not that anything was wrong.

Our hardships are relieved somewhat by the presence of a swimming pool in the front yard: Lake Eyre, a huge salt lake. We spend half the day lying in it. It's very shallow, but we've found a place where we can get all the way underwater. We roll back and forth a little, like languid elephants with hats on. Using our tent and the branches of a dead tree that's standing in the lake, we made a lean-to beside the car. I'm sitting there now. I've taught Monique how to play gin-rummy, and she's better at it than you are. But then I think she's learned to read the backs of the cards. It's a greasy, old deck.

I didn't dump you because of any *love* for her. She's that Belgian girl I told you about one time, the first girl I ever went to bed with, when I was seventeen, and who broke up with me straight afterwards with a note saying it had been a joke. I didn't find out what kind of joke until I got here, but that's probably been on TV in Holland as well. I could have figured she was a bitch, and fallen in love with the next one, but I used her to choose my character, and let her become the idea of love. Is she nice? Do I like her? None of that matters. I was with her thirty years ago for that one day, and in Sydney, when I got the chance to remain faithful to that day, to the Jacques I've become through her, I did it. There was no choice, the way a child has to go with its parents, the way a ghost has to haunt the house it's given.

I have no idea what drives her. Back then I wrote her desperate letters, and she wrote back to say that she read them aloud to her friends, so they could make fun of me. She was so hostile that I almost didn't dare to visit her in Sydney. But from the first moment it was as though I was the only thing in her life. She's lost a staggering fortune, and she's afraid of losing me. I don't understand it.

What I also don't understand is that I haven't let you know anything. That is deeply mean. Maybe it's because Monica and I had to be together, but I couldn't take the two of us seriously as a couple, a couple that exists in reality. Like I was dreaming her, and had to keep her safe by not waking up.

I'm not trying to say it wasn't mean.

Four-thirty. In half an hour we start our death march. Our cans and water bottles are cooling in the lake. We'll get to the Oodnadatta Track around seven, and there will still be an hour or two of light. After that we'll have no chance of getting a ride; people don't drive roads like these after dark.

All the guidebooks about the Australian outback advise you, in the event of a breakdown, to stay by your car and die there. We could take turns going to the road. But Monica doesn't like to sit still. She wants to walk, and so we'll walk.

We've got fifteen hours before the heat becomes unbearable tomorrow morning. Monica thinks that will give us enough time to get so close to William Creek that we'll be able to do the rest in that heat. Nonsense, we'd have to average six kilometers an hour all night. Five seems like the maximum to me. That gives us plenty of time to burn alive tomorrow. We're just too far away from the world to be able to get any closer by walking. And if we do make it – William Creek has a population of two. What if they aren't home?

Monica has gone down to the lake to fish out our cans. I'm going to take a dip as well. Then I'll put this letter in my pocket, and become a walking bottle with a message for you.

How are you doing? Has old Jack Frost returned to Holland yet? I'm scared.

Jacques.

10

At the top of a rise they took a last look at the Fairmont: a little white cube, far away by the blue water, almost camouflaged against the salty crust.

It was just past six-thirty when they reached the Oodnadatta Track, lying red, stony and endless before them. They walked quickly, intently, not talking much; after days of doing nothing by the lake, Jacques found the movement invigorating. He enjoyed the rhythm of his steps, his breath like a pinwheel in his lungs, the soft sweat on his forehead. He could walk forever. It was like the Boy Scout marches when he was a boy: it cost no effort, but you were still a hero who had done something unimaginable.

Every half-hour they paused for a moment and drank something. Car tires and the occasional burned-out wreck broke the walk into stages; a vertical white object was good for fifteen minutes of curiosity about what it might be, and when they saw that it was an old refrigerator, about what had last been in it.

Beer, Monique reckoned.

The sun went down, the hope of a car vanished. A sea of stars came up, the darkness hid the tires, and finally there was nothing left to show that they were moving forward. They had to keep a close eye on the edges of the road, to make sure they didn't wander off into the bush. The sky was an immeasurable dome all around them, and at the same time everything was little and cozy and close, like an attic room. Monique was a white shadow, sometimes in front, sometimes beside him. There was no sound, only that of their footsteps and the tinkling of the cans in their backpacks.

If he survived, he would remember this walk as the closest he had been to Monique. It was her! – it was still impossible to believe, but she was the girl he had seen at Oppy's. He had walked up to her, asked her to dance, and their step toward the dance floor had brought them here. There had been nothing in between.

MONIQUE WAS BUSY SINGING all the Madame Twenty jingles she could remember when Jacques saw it: a vague glow, behind them. He told her to stop. It was eleven-thirty. The glow shuddered, became a light that moved, two lights, two dancing headlights.

'A car,' Monique said. 'It's going to drive past us. It's on a different track.'

In the desert Jacques had been reminded before of his father's story about how, as a boy, he had been playing in a railroad yard when he saw a train coming at him. He had waited, paralyzed with fear, to see whether it was on his track. This was the opposite; the oncoming car had to save their lives. Roads like the Oodnadatta Track had a way of splitting up into countless side roads that didn't go anywhere, but just ran beside the real road for a while, sometimes for dozens of kilometers, then merged with it again. Those extra roads had been created by drivers, maybe camel drivers too, who had been maddened by always following the same road, and had driven into the void, followed later by copycats. Sometimes 'the road' was four or five parallel roads, all far apart. The car that could save them might drive by without even seeing them.

But it stopped at their feet, high on its wheels, shaking like a big, dumb animal; a jeep with a roo bar sturdy enough to knock a lost cow off the road. Jacques felt a twinge of disappointment: now he'd never know how it would have ended if that jeep hadn't shown up.

Rick Wyndham, the forty-six-year-old tax inspector from Marree who climbed out of the jeep, had gotten into an argument on the phone earlier that evening with

116

his girlfriend in Coober Pedy, and had decided to go straight to her and talk things out, 375 kilometers be damned. He had a black beard, a dense mess of curly hair, bare feet in thongs, and thick glasses through which he looked at them questioningly. 'I'm totally pissed,' he said. 'Is that okay? Doesn't really matter, if you go off the road here you don't even notice till a hundred kilometers further.'

He thundered on, foot to the floor, much, much faster than Jacques and Monique had ever dared to drive these roads by daylight, swerving, tossed left and right by potholes, sometimes right over the edge of the road, and still keeping the jeep under control. William Creek was two barracks and one light and gone again, stones slammed against the chassis like cannonballs, and inside everything jiggled and tinkled along, heaps of tools, jerrycans, the empty beer cans Rick tossed over his shoulder, burping loudly and without apology.

Jacques asked him whether they had really been in danger, and Rick roared with laughter. 'The way we fight? I've driven halfway around the globe already for that girl; only thing you have to watch out for on the Oodnadatta Track is that I don't run over you. No, mate, the pioneering days are over. Hey. Do you mind if I guess your ages? You're fifty. And you're forty-seven. How do I know that? Because you're Madame Twenty, and you're that Dutch quizmaster. Don't you read the papers?'

'Not many newsstands out at Lake Eyre,' Monique said.

Half an hour after the two of them had walked out of the Oodnadatta Inn in Marree, Rick had come in for a beer. The place had been humming with Madame Twenty and the TV program with which she and her Dutch friend had given themselves away. It had taken a while before the police were notified – Australians were no great tattletales – but in the days after that their photos, the license number of their car, police drawings and descriptions of what they looked like now had been on all the channels and in all the papers. The robbery had saved them; if they hadn't bivouacked in the bush for a few days, they would definitely have been caught by now. They couldn't show their faces anywhere anymore, at least not together. That night they could sleep at his girlfriend's, but after that . . .

'I've been figuring,' Rick said after fifty kilometers of silence. 'I saved you guys. Suppose you do something for me. Eileen's got a daughter in Brisbane, Vera. She works for the *Brisbane Courier*. Give her an interview. It'd be the chance of a lifetime, and it'll get me in good forever with Eileen. It's a girl you can trust one hundred percent. Think about it.'

'I already have,' Monique said. 'That newspaper can't afford it. An interview with me is worth at least fifty thousand. I'll pay your girlfriend for her trouble, okay?'

'Oh, all right,' Rick said.

After William Creek the road was only loose sand, and the jeep careened back and forth between the low, sandy shoulders on both sides. Rick seemed to be sleeping, awoken occasionally by his own deep belches. Monique sat close to Jacques, her hand on his leg or in his hand.

Beneath the stars, lights appeared: Coober Pedy. Money for an interview: so she still hadn't given up. But Jacques wasn't going any further – Coober Pedy was the end of the line.

AT HALF PAST TWO Rick stopped in the front yard of Eileen's house, a bungalow at the edge of town. He went in, and came back a little later. Behind him, a fat, white, jouncing ghost in a nightie came out and stood in the doorway: Eileen. Jacques could barely keep from laughing when he saw how ugly the loved one was for whom Rick had passionately driven so many kilometers. She was furious; looking back on it, they should have anticipated that: waking your girlfriend in the middle of the night with two strangers you'd said could sleep in her house wasn't much of a way to make up. Even if they *were* castaways rescued from the desert, fuck off! Even if one of them *was* Madame Twenty, fuck the hell off! Finally they were allowed in, but only if they promised to leave first thing in the morning. And Rick needn't have any illusions about sleeping in her bedroom.

The three of them were assigned to the junk room, with a couple of mattresses on the floor. Rick fell asleep right away, breathing so deeply it was almost snoring, and spreading sour alcohol fumes. The fan on the ceiling peeped and growled, but the heat was as steady as tar.

EILEEN HAD A GIRLFRIEND in Cabramatta whose husband had lost his job when Seawear fell apart. But, undaunted by Eileen's hatred, Monique ran down the list right away: first, the court had acquitted her, so it wasn't all that simple; second, as it turned out, the woman wasn't really a friend, but an acquaintance of an acquaintance; and thirdly: how would Eileen like to make a little easy money? While Jacques looked on flabbergasted, they actually started negotiating: for nine percent of what Monique would get for an interview, with a minimum of four thousand dollars, they could stay one more night and a day. Until the next evening at seven, because then Eileen had her bridge club.

And at once, Monique went on negotiating, on the phone now, with papers and magazines in Sydney and Melbourne. It was fascinating, here at the very last, to watch her do what her life must have been, and what, after her arrest and imprisonment, would undoubtedly in some way be her life again. She always mentioned her name, kept talking straight through the bafflement that must have produced at the other end, and asked to speak to someone she knew, usually the editor-in-chief. 'Hi, Monica George here . . . yeah, long time no see . . . what would you pay for an interview with me?' It sounded like an invitation to a birthday party, as though she had to hurry a bit because she had a hundred other people to call. After playing off a couple of old acquaintances against each other, her interview went for forty-five thousand dollars to *Fact*, a Melbourne weekly. And when the last call was over, she put down the phone with a triumphant smile. All fixed. From a hopeless position, she was back in the game.

THAT AFTERNOON THEY BORROWED Rick's jeep; he and Eileen still had to make up, and there was no way *she* was leaving *her* house.

The town rattled and jangled with draglines, monsters with outstretched claws, and old pickups, many carrying signs atop the cab that said they were transporting dynamite. They ended up in a landscape of whitish grit cones, rooted up by diggers in search of opals. Amid a far stretch of abandoned mines they climbed out. They had to watch their step, the old shafts weren't fenced off. Broken planks and buttress beams were lying strewn about, and there were still signs hammered into the earth that bore the numbers and names of hopeful diggers who had once held claim to these plots. They scrambled up a cone and looked out over landscape pocked as though the earth here had some kind of skin disease, and which stretched out all the way to the jagged horizon. From far away came the roar and rattle of draglines at mines that were still operating.

When would he say it? Where did this awful fear come from, the fear of doing to her what she had done so many times worse to him? He already *had* said it, in Marree, but she had acted as though that had been a meaningless outburst of rage, as if it had been no more than a slap in the face.

He couldn't leave her alone now. She had to get her money for the interview first.

When they came down off their pimple, Monique leaping like a child down a dune, she went and stood at the edge of a shaft, forcing into Jacques' mind the push that would make her disappear.

'Or shall I just jump?' she said.

RICK AND EILEEN WERE sitting in front of the TV, unhappy and glum, but Monique made her calls right through it all, this time in search of a hideaway. She called friends and acquaintances all over Australia, as if she'd seen them only yesterday, seemingly unaware of the desperation it showed. A few days ago she would have let Jacques call, now she made a hundred calls herself; someone, somewhere, must have been tapping the conversations. And even if one of her contacts did have something for her, mightn't there be people involved who would turn her in?

In the middle of a call, the TV screen suddenly showed – also to the person she had on the line – their battered Fairmont at its spot along Lake Eyre. A mail plane had spotted it that afternoon for the second time in the last few days; the police had gone to look and found the car with which Madame Twenty had been sighted in Marree. A second set of tire tracks suggested that they had switched cars at Lake Eyre – although that made it a mystery why the Fairmont had been wrecked. Food wrappers they'd left behind indicated that they had camped for a few days at that spot; the police had probably arrived just a little too late.

Eileen was terrified Monique would be found in her house.

LYNN KUKLOVSKI OF *Fact*, a robust, unattractive girl, was carrying forty-five thousand dollars and a receipt for

Monique to sign. The interview took place in the living room, with Eileen and Rick sitting there, and it was amazingly dull. Most of it had to do with the demise of Madame Twenty, the fraud, the channeling of funds, the tax evasion, the Seawear Affair. And while Eileen rolled her eyes and sniffed, to express a disgust at such practices that Jacques felt as well, Monique answered each question with verve. He was surprised at the pains she took to justify her own actions, and to put the blame on Wolpe. What did it matter? That was all far behind her now – what did the butterfly care that the caterpillar had once been wronged? – what did Lynn Kuklovski, or her readers, care about how the tax department had been diddled, now that a fairy-tale figure, someone who existed only in people's minds anymore, was sitting right in front of her?

Occasionally, when talk turned to one scam or another, Monique beamed at him, and that caused him pain, as if she was a girl showing you her picture albums after you had already stopped loving her. She described the route they'd taken, confirmed and denied sightings, gave detailed descriptions of the robbers at Lake Eyre, but not a single answer, and not a single question either, displayed any insight into the absurdity of having vanished, of the grandeur and wretchedness of Wolpe's end, the loss of love with that man. It was as though Jacques were reading her diary of their trip, and while Lynn Kuklovski's tapes ran full with talk that was in no way value for her money, and he watched with compassion as Rick made tea and passed out cups and cookies, tripping continually when his left flip-flop popped its thong, his consternation grew at the hollowness with which Monique had experienced the sweet and the bitter they had shared.

Suddenly, Lynn Kuklovski asked: 'How did you and Jacques meet, anyway?'

And in front of this perfect stranger Lynn, of Eileen and Rick, of the millions who were listening, in front of *him*, Monique told in peculiar detail and from a peculiar bird's-eye view about Ostend, as if that was a beach resort and not Holy Ground. Oh, she and Jacques had met there during a vacation. They had talked, danced, fallen madly in love, and on the boulevard they'd had a picture taken, a picture she'd often looked at later. A summer idyll. But a seventeen-year-old schoolboy and a twenty-year-old secretary, of course that could never work out. They'd written to each other for a while, and then that had faded. That's the way those things went. 'But he made quite an impression on me!' That business about Christa – true, they knew each other from gymnastics contests, and she had been his pen-pal first, but that hadn't really played a role: back then, everyone went to Ostend, how could she have known that she would run into Jacques herself? The story about it being a joke must have been something Christa had dreamed up later, because she was jealous. And now that fate had given them a second chance they would never let each other go again. A fairy tale.

'Isn't that right, Jack?'

'Yes,' he said, and he saw Sonja, holding a Dutch newspaper with that line.

RICK HAD LEFT WITHOUT Eileen saying goodbye, and was now somewhere out on the Oodnadatta Track, Lynn Kuklovski was flying back to Melbourne with her worthless interview, and Eileen was at her bridge club. For eight hundred dollars she was letting them stay one more night, but they had to be out before ten the next morning. And while it grew dark outside, Monique went on phoning bit players from her life, carefully edging up to the core of it: the gardener, a script girl, an assistant manager, her daughters' old boyfriends. No one had a place for her, and finally the only ones left were her daughters and her ex-husband. Howard George said something that shocked her and made her drop the receiver, while an angry, metallic voice talked on. Her youngest daughter started crying, and after a cordial word to the husband of her oldest daughter, something happened that made her slam down the phone herself.

She laughed, leaned back in her chair and said: 'End of the road for Madame Twenty.'

And now he must say it. It was as if he'd be so unmasked that there would be nothing left of him.

She came over and sat beside him, with that slightly apologetic smile he remembered from Batemans Bay, when she had come to bed with him for the first time. So *she* was the one who was going to say it. But now that the adventure had come to an end, he wanted to earn that end by having done everything to make it last. And in his mind he saw an image of a young man he had talked to for a while in the washhouse of a campground long ago, a fellow from Brisbane who made his living by fixing up abandoned farms and renting them out as holiday homes. In one smooth motion he found Marcus Eboli in his notebook, Monique called him and it turned out Eboli had a place in Queensland they could go to right away.

Monique took Jacques' hand and led him to the junk room, to the mattresses. No one would be going to Eboli. The telephone call had been a demonstration of fighting spirit, idle proof that the adventure could be stretched even further. But it was finished. This was the last, the very last, and it was happening now. And perhaps for the first time since Ostend, they took off *each other's* clothes, shy and clumsy. Jacques was afraid he was going to cry, and that she would too, and suddenly the door flew open and the light went on.

'You pigs,' Eileen said. There was a furious calm in her voice. 'Get out of my house.' She stood in the doorway, big and fat and hating.

'Goddamn it,' Monique said. 'Can't you see we're fucking? Piss off, this is our room, I paid eight hundred dollars for it.'

'You'll get your money back,' Eileen said. 'Out.'

'You can't put us out on the street in the middle of the night.'

'It's eleven o'clock. The hotels are open. Get out.'

'We'll leave tomorrow.'

'Oh you will?' Eileen said. She walked away, her hate remained hanging. Monique got up, turned off the light and closed the door and lay down beside Jacques again, but a moment later the angry footsteps were back, and the door flew open again. The light went on, and Eileen pointed a rifle at them.

'Out,' she said. 'Now.'

'All right,' Monique said, 'all right.' She sat up, leaned over and picked up the black backpack beside the mattress, as if it contained the 'getting out' which she would now produce. She pulled out her pistol, molded her hand to it like a racecar driver adjusting his helmet, and fired.

THEY SAID NOTHING AND drove, their faces lit in stripes by the dashboard of Eileen's car, with the same swarm of little white insects in the headlights all the way to Alice Springs. A seven-hundred kilometer drive, further than Amsterdam–Paris, but in Australia a trip made in an evening, a night.

When they changed places they looked at each other across the roof of the car – a deep, gripping, completely desperate moment. Jacques couldn't grasp what had happened. Only an hour, two hours ago he hadn't been a murderer, he had been counting the nights until he would be in Amsterdam. Now he still wasn't a murderer, but with one twitch of her index finger Monique had wiped it all away, filled the night with invisible police-men, years in prison, letters he would write to Sonja from his cell. So it goes that fast, a murder, he had thought while Eileen crumpled, an amazement in her eyes that gave her face something nice for the first time. At a flash he had admired Monique for the pertinence of the shot, the snappy answer it was. But he had seen a person being killed! That had really happened! And every time that sank in, he thought: now I'll never make it home, and then he saw the look Monique had given him, an ice-cold look that had said: you watch your step.

THEY GOT TO THE airport at Alice Springs at seven in the morning. There was a flight to Brisbane at eleven; they bought their tickets separately, and drove around until check-in time. Separate taxis took them back to the airport, where they stayed as far away from each other as possible. Jacques felt like he was an unstoppable alarm screaming 'murder', but nothing happened. One time he caught Monique's eye, and despite his misery he almost had to laugh at what her look said: Chin up! We'll make it! A: want it, B: do it!

They should have gone to the police in Coober Pedy, and that would still be the wisest thing to do, but Monique had wanted something else, and Jacques was too tired, too dirty, too lost to kick up a fuss. She had to say what was going to happen, or else the police; he didn't care anymore. At Eileen's house he had shaved his beard back to a moustache, and Monique had put on the wig of long, wavy, reddish-brown hair she'd brought with her from the Fairmont, but caution couldn't help them anymore; they were in the hands of chance.

In the plane he was surrounded by passengers who were everything he wasn't; people with normal-people plans, on their way to other people just like themselves.

130

He sat beside Marjorie Crown, a seventeen-year-old girl with a sweet, innocent face, whose Big Day it was; that evening she would start her first job, as a waitress at a floating hotel on the Gold Coast south of Brisbane. It was as though his voice no longer had the strength to rise up out of him, as though he had to pull his words up from the bottom of a coal mine, and he prayed that he would never steal the unforgettableness of this day from her; that she would never find out that she had been sitting beside a murderer on the lam.

He was still hanging on to the world by his fingertips, ready to let go.

AT FOUR O'CLOCK THEY climbed out of a bus in the center of Brisbane. In the entrance to a parking garage they spoke for a moment. Monique would try to get hold of Eboli and to buy a car; if all went well, she would pick up Jacques at a little park by the river, Battery Park, which she'd marked on a folder from the plane. And if things didn't go well, they would meet up some other way. With a little wave she vanished into the afternoon crowd.

NEVER SINCE HE HAD first entered Leichhardt Street had he been this long without her. He spent hours sitting on benches, watching children rocking back and forth on playground animals, an Aboriginal family sitting on the grass in a circle, children playing soccer in real soccer jerseys, green against yellow. Occasionally he nodded off, amazed to find when he awoke that the children were still rocking and playing ball, that the murder was still there.

In Holland the papers would call him a murderer too. Still, he had to go back there, he still could. He could simply walk away and buy a ticket. He could also go to the police. It had been self-defense; they must have found Eileen with the rifle in her hand. And all he had done was sit there! If he turned himself in now, he might get away with one year, two years at most, and maybe he'd be allowed to serve them in Holland.

But he couldn't move.

HE WOKE UP. The soccer players were gone, the playground animals rocked gently under their own weight. At the end of a path was Monique, younger than he remembered her, in a clean white T-shirt and a new pair of jeans. He got up and walked over to her, knowing that his last chance was now being lost, but at least there was a will that moved him, even if it wasn't his own. She walked in front of him, out of the park, he climbed into a car she had waiting there and, the next morning, after a drive that made him feel like a bare wheel being scraped across cobblestones, they stopped in a quiet forest, at the edge of a river.

There was a rowboat, and they rowed to the other side. Through some trees they could see a light-green field of grass that sloped up gently to a little yellow house with a gray roof; the house Monique had rented from Marcus Eboli, the only habitation within ten kilometers: Fort Madness.

They began walking up the grassy slope. Beside a bathtub on lion's feet, a trough for animals that must once have grazed here, was a tap. They opened it: brownish water came out, and they tossed it over their heads and arms and it tasted sweet to their lips, like forest.

Where to from here? As far as plans went: nowhere.

11

T HE NEXT MORNING she came crawling into his tent. She had her overnight bag with her, a sack of fresh rolls, and a ballpoint with the emblem of Ostend, to write his books with. They'd been planning to go for a swim, but they stayed in his tent and she missed her train, and the next two as well. A transistor radio in a neighboring tent played hits, they heard the trams and cars passing along the sea embankment, they ate the rolls and lay in each other's arms unforgettably. The afternoon in Brussels loomed up occasionally. It had only been a week ago, with Christa there on the sofa. Christa had been obliterated, or, rather, he himself was obliterated from her world of chastity and reverence, in which a girl like Monique simply didn't exist; a completely naked girl who pressed herself against you, sighing and blushing with pleasure.

This was different, more gentle, sweeter than at the

hotel. Only now did he notice how hectic that had been; the bed wasn't allowed to creak, the proprietress could knock at any moment, and the realization that he was actually going to bed with a girl had only sunk in when he was back down the fire escape and standing on the street.

They went for a swim after all and, missing more and more trains, walked back along the beach and boulevard to Ostend. Colorful kites flapped in the wind, some soccer players shouted to her. This was the Walk of Walks, it was for this that Ostend had been built, that the earth revolved. The sun shone and he was seventeen and the most wonderful girl in the world hung on his neck and let the cafés, the entire boulevard see that they had Fucked until they couldn't do it anymore. Now they should forget all the rest and climb onto his moped and head into the wide world, never to return. He said it, and Monique laughed and changed it into a new date, for the next Saturday in Ostend. In front of the casino was a photographer, and she and Jacques posed at the balustrade, their arms around each other, and had him take a picture. She ordered two prints and asked Jacques to send one to her office in Brussels.

'But you'll be here on Saturday, right?'

'Then I'll have it sooner.'

'Stay here, then you'll get it sooner still.'

'I have to work, Jack.'

'Typing other people's letters. Come on, we'll go to Paris. We'll be there by tomorrow.'

'And who's going to earn the money?'

She laughed and kissed him, and in the Saskatchewan afternoon club on Langestraat they danced to 'I'm Sorry' by Brenda Lee. Monique sang along softly, her arms around his waist, her head on his shoulder, and she punched the number in two more times on the jukebox.

They'd known each other for less than a day, but they already had a song that was *their* song.

WHEN HE HAD BROUGHT her to the train, and went to Oppy's later that evening, the place was empty; nothing but a room with people in it. He did something new: before closing time, he went back to his tent. There he found Monique's scent, the crumbs from her rolls. Through the tent cloth he saw the spots of light from cars along the embankment. Where were the cars that had driven there while Monique was here? The idea that those cars would never again all be together suddenly made him incredibly sad.

12

F ROM THE THINKING rock, as Monique called it, and
which she had accepted as a place only he was
allowed to come, Jacques had a view over all of Fort
Madness. It was the highest point you could reach on an
otherwise unscalably steep rock wall that formed the
western perimeter; a little plateau where he could sit
with his back against the rock, his legs dangling over the
edge — a place created to serve as a lookout over the
whole property.

To the right was the impenetrable bush, low shrubs,
and trees with bright white trunks, stretching for kilometers to the southern border; a far bend of the same
rock wall. To the left, audible but invisible, was the
waterfall. A bit further along, brown and turbulent and
with little rainbows above it when the sun shone, the
Yorty appeared, only to disappear again a little later
behind the stand of eucalyptus. That was where the

rowboat was moored – hidden as well somewhere on the other shore was the gray Holden. Much further along, the Yorty curved to the right and became the eastern limit of Fort Madness. Directly in front of him, tiny from his high and distant post, was the house, beside it the corrugated-iron water tank. Past that, in the hazy distance, was the sea. Sometimes he imagined he could see it, but the sea was four hundred kilometers away.

It really was called Fort Madness, at least: above the door was a plank with big, optimistic letters on it, almost bleached away now by the sun. But in a country where Lake Disappointment and Mount Hopeless were official geographical names, it should perhaps come as no surprise that the original residents, a group of idealistic young people from Brisbane, had given that name to the old farm where they had hoped to establish a new life. There had been eight of them, two couples with two young children each, and the project had failed: within three years they had moved back to Brisbane.

Not so much because it really *had* been madness – Australia had not been ripe for the zucchini and capers on which they'd hoped to base their livelihood – but because something else had stopped them. Ten kilometers above Fort Madness was an old dam in the river, which was to be replaced with a much bigger one, ten kilometers downstream; what they had so lovingly cultivated was the bottom of a lake: Lake Yorty.

The state had expropriated Fort Madness for a good price, and granted them the right to use the land until the new dam was finished and the valley would have to be evacuated. That could take years, but the spirit was gone and they had left as quickly as possible, leaving Fort Madness to the acquaintance who had helped them to make it habitable: Marcus Eboli. Marcus had installed a generator, a fridge and a television set, in order to rent it out as a holiday home, but that had never happened: it was too far away from everything. Until Monique called; for seven thousand dollars she had rented Fort Madness until the end of its days – whenever that might be.

HE HAD ONLY A few thoughts on the thinking rock, always the same ones. There was a calculation he made over and over again and which showed that he and Sonja never slept at the same time, and were only awake simultaneously for eight hours of any given day, two hours in the morning and six hours in the evening. He wanted to leave. But he couldn't leave. It had all gotten incredibly out of hand. His plane had been delayed, and just to kill time he had gone to look at the house of an old girlfriend. That was all! Now he was months down the road, looking out over the valley in which he was locked up with her, a pair of cowardly killers, wanted all over the country. Again and always he saw the look on Eileen's face at the moment she had crumpled, crestfallen, like the face of a child from whom you've taken away a pencil it was using to scribble in a book. The shot had become a word, with a way to spell it: BLAM, as though Monique's pistol had been one of those toy ones that produced a flag with that word. Eileen's death didn't bother him, he didn't even care about having done nothing: she had been a nasty, ugly person who deserved to be dead. He found her a bit ridiculous, with that dying of hers: like an April Fool's victim who didn't know she had a fish hanging on her back. The laughable ignorance of those who die unexpectedly! The living became their Peeping Toms, saw them lathering a face they'd never get to shave, putting on a bathing cap their corpse would wear, jotting down appointments for the day of their funeral. And the clothes they wore! Would a death-row convict ever choose to be executed in the floral dress in which Eileen, rifle in hand, had come stomping into their junk room in the final minute of her life?

But Jacques couldn't shake the thought of Rick. Good old, nearsighted Rick with his broken flip-flop who had driven back and forth through the desert, drinking and belching, crazy with sleep, just to make up with that fucking bitch, and who had heard back in Marree that the most precious thing in his life was dead, murdered by the people he had brought into her home.

One of Rick's moments kept coming back to Jacques, the moment of his departure. Eileen hadn't even walked him to the door, and by chance Jacques had stood there with him himself, knowing suddenly that this was the moment at which Rick's jeep could save him. But Rick had mumbled something unintelligible and walked outside, completely stunned by Eileen's attitude, and Jacques had not gone with him.

And then he saw the murder again, and instead of Eileen's look he saw Monique's – and he knew that she had done it to keep him from getting away.

THE FIRST FEW DAYS it was like having no skin. Every noise could be that of helicopters that would come buzzing over Fort Madness the next moment, of bullhorns by the river ordering them to give themselves up. They couldn't turn on the TV without seeing the bungalow in Coober Pedy, or their Fairmont at Lake Eyre, or Eileen, or Rick, broken, weeping with indignation.

Jacques suggested that they turn themselves in together. If they played it right, they could probably get off with relatively light sentences. But she took him in her arms, as though his suggestion were a moment of weakness and deserving of comfort. The thought of giving herself up had occurred to her too on occasion, but those were precisely the moments when they needed to support each other. 'At the first obstacle, half the world gives up; at the second obstacle, the other half gives up. The third obstacle is where we get started, Jack.'

Could she say something like that and really mean it? It wasn't even original, he knew that phrase of hers, he'd read it in some tabloid.

But if they didn't give themselves up, what then?

'Do you remember, in Ostend?' Monique said.

'I remember everything about Ostend.'

'So do I. And you don't know what I was thinking. Remember we walked along the boulevard, from the campground into town, and you said we should go away together?'

'You laughed at me.'

'Of course I laughed at you. But in my mind I saw where we would go. Here. This is paradise.'

Jacques had a gruesome vision: Fort Madness really was paradise. Outside was nothing.

AFTER A WEEK THEY needed to do some shopping; Monique went. To keep from being recognized by each other's company, only one of them could be seen, always the same one, and she made it seem obvious that she had to be that one.

Once she was gone, the gonging loneliness made Jacques reel. What to do when there's nothing to do? Where to stay, without her as the focal point of his longing to be free of her? In the bedroom he looked through her things. A couple of pairs of panties and vests, a cap, a little bag with vials and brushes. No passport, no money, no pistol.

He looked in the kitchen cupboards, under the beds, in the bathroom, in rooms they didn't use, in out-buildings, afraid of finding something where she must have hidden it from him. He found nothing, and went to the thinking rock, but climbed right back down again; the seclusion there was unbearable, now that it was no longer seclusion from her. Suddenly he was seized by a fearful hunch and ran back to the house, but his money and his two passports were still in the side pocket of his backpack. He took them out, and in one of the out-buildings he wrapped them up in a piece of plastic, along with a toy flashlight he'd found, and tucked them behind a pile of corrugated-iron sheets.

After that he didn't know what to do.

He walked back down to the river. The rowboat was on the far shore, and he waded through the water that came up to his waist. He felt like a child who has gone through a forbidden garden gate; it was the first time since they'd been at Fort Madness that he had left the property.

He started following the track; an hour later the woods parted and he was standing beside a telegraph pole, at the crossing with a broader gravel path. This was where the world began, people came here. He waited for a few minutes, ready to jump back into the trees, but no one came and he started to walk back. In any case, the walk had been a good idea: an hour had passed, and before he was back at Fort Madness, where waiting was all he could do, another hour would be gone.

He decided not to tell Monique about his escapade.

In another corner of the same outbuilding where he had hidden his packet, behind a pile of rusty farm equipment, he found a ball. He took it outside; it was a Mickey Mouse ball, gone soft, the paint weathered. The child who had lost the ball must have been mad with sorrow, but precisely because it must have forgotten that sorrow long ago, Jacques felt desperately sorrowful. He looked up, hoping to at least see a plane, but the sky was empty. Later one came floating over, high and silent, like a fossil in glass.

He thought: I'll never get back home.

SHE CAME BACK, delighted that it had worked, went again a week later, came back again, went again. And

144

every time Jacques waded to the other side and walked to the telegraph pole, and beyond. One time he saw a phone booth. But he had no coins, and the impossibility of getting any made him feel more hopelessly cut off than ever. Another time he saw a couple of people close to a shed, two adults working on a boat, *Le Frog*, which was lying on its side, and a child hopping around in the grass as if trying to catch a fly. The image of those people, real people, stayed with him for days.

In time Jacques began longing for Monique's shopping forays, because of the walks he took then, but also because of the way his loneliness lifted when she returned. He liked her well enough, it wasn't that. But it was impossible to keep this up, this being beside her, with her, in her, with a head full of getting away from here. They fucked almost every night, silently, almost industriously, and always with Jacques wresting from himself amazement at having this girl in his arms again.

She never said 'say something sweet' anymore.

During the day he would sit on his thinking rock or wander around, stamping his feet, kicking at stones, his heart sewed up in the soles of old shoes. Fort Madness was quiet, and poignantly pretty. It smelled of thyme, the grass was brown and crunchy beneath his feet, with bleached Lego blocks and half pairs of pliers among the leaves. Trees rustled, deer, foxes, kangaroos came poking around, in the bushes kookaburras cackled. A few times he saw a fat, black snake shoot off. There was a half-collapsed playhouse on stilts that had belonged to the children who had lived here, fallen fences still strung with rusty barbed wire, and on a line hung the clothespins from a final wash. On top of a little hill was an old stove with a beautifully embellished turquoise oven door, like a fortress to be taken on the island that would be there someday.

The longer Jacques stayed at Fort Madness, the more time he was willing to spend in prison in order not to have to be there. But she didn't want to leave, and if he went alone then *he* had committed the murder, he had no doubt about that.

And if he ran for it anyway? Then he would at least need the car. But he never saw the keys to the Holden. Why didn't she just leave them in the fruit bowl when she was at home? Was she less sure of herself than she seemed, did she want to make it harder for him to escape? One time, while she was swimming by the waterfall, he looked in her handbag, and in the black backpack. No keys, no pistol.

Only days afterwards, while he was sitting on the thinking rock and she was doing her fitness exercises in the little field in front of the house, did it occur to him that maybe she simply left the keys in the ignition. He climbed down right away, walked to the river, and rowed to the other side.

There was nothing in the ignition.

Through the trees he saw Monique, and she saw him. What was he going to say if she asked what he'd been doing at the car?

'Jack!' she shouted. She waved.

'Monique!'

'Jack! I love you!'

SOMETIMES HE THOUGHT about killing her. Rusty metal objects enough in the sheds with which to bash in her brains while she slept. But he wouldn't do it: she hadn't earned the right to have pushed him that far.

There was one redeeming thought: the deluge. One day they would have to leave Fort Madness. They didn't know when. It could be months, years.

NOTHING CHANGED ANYMORE. The police didn't come, Marcus Eboli didn't come, it rained, then stopped raining, the fledglings flew from their nest in the hole in the wall. Fort Madness seemed like a forgotten world, separated from the real one by an invisible wall with only one leak: the television set. The swimming matches, cooking lessons, train accidents that poured

147

in through that leak were like pictures in a history book, scenes from civilizations beyond reach. Occasionally the local station had something about the dam – cranes piled concrete blocks, the governor of Queensland came for a look in a yellow hard hat, a bulldozer rolled into a ravine and killed the driver. They themselves disappeared from the screen, out of the papers Monique brought with her: they had disappeared inside their own disappearance.

Monique did all the housekeeping, including filling the gas engine of the pump by the river, and that of the generator. They sat on the porch swing, they swam, she suggested a Fort Madness Absolute Gin-Rummy Championship, and when he asked how many rounds it would have, she said: 'A million.'

Under a bookcase Jacques found a Monopoly game containing a notepad with the scores of an unfinished game between S., G. and Zippy. One day he overcame his shame, set up the game and played on for all three. It was as though, by building upon a real past, he was taking part in something that actually existed. For a while he finished that game almost every day, always hoping Zippy would win, and happy whenever that happened. He didn't know whether Zippy had been a man or a woman, a boy or a girl, but he imagined it to be the child he had seen near the boat *Le Frog*.

The hours he slept kept growing longer, and the days

kept passing more easily, and in greater quantities. The flies buzzed, he couldn't see Sonja's face very clearly anymore, he forgot about the car keys. He became so drowsy that he sometimes wondered whether Monique was slipping him narcotics. And when he raised himself from his lethargy once to find out what he thought of himself now, he discovered to his dismay that he was in the process of becoming happy at Fort Madness.

ONE DAY JACQUES SAW a human being. He was down by the river when he heard the sound of a car on the other side. An uneven, rattling sound, he knew right away it couldn't be the police, but he hid anyway and a few moments later a battered and weathered Ford Falcon came down the rutted track. He followed it at a safe distance, and watched from behind some bushes as a young man climbed out, looked around and shouted something a few times, then finally nailed an envelope to a tree and drove off.

It was a letter from the Queensland Water Resources Commission, and it said that the valley would be flooded in five weeks' time. Two weeks before that, three weeks from now, Fort Madness had to be evacuated.

Jacques saw the boat *Le Frog* where the child Zippy had played, and understood only now: it was being fixed up in order to go boating here.

Monique was on the porch, looking out over the grassy hillside to the river. Jacques handed her the letter, and when she had read it she nodded. She looked at him and said what he suddenly knew she would say – what he had always known she would say when this moment came, the grisly elegance, the macabre sensibility of which was inevitable: 'I'm staying.'

13

T HE LADY AT the camera store found his pictures, glanced at them, and handed them to him with a smile.

'You're a lucky young man,' she said.

They were leaning against the balustrade at the casino, arms around each other, heads together, behind them bathers and waders who would never know they were in this picture. Monique was smiling with her eyes open, he had his half closed, and you could see everything, what it had been like in the tent, how much in love they were, that they belonged together forever.

He walked along the boulevard and wondered where everyone found the strength to live without Monique Ilegems. And what kind of nonsense was that, waiting till Saturday — what would she think of him if he left it up to a *postman* to deliver the photo, a photo like this!

All he had was the name of the place where she

worked in Brussels, Camita, and a post office box number, but the Brussels phone book at the post office listed only one Camita, and he called them.

At first the lady who answered didn't want to put him through; employees were not to take personal calls. Only when he said that it was extremely urgent did she do it.

He almost didn't recognize her. She didn't seem at all pleased to be hearing from him so soon, and she actually didn't want him to bring the photo in person. It was a long way, she had no time, in the evenings she had her training. He almost had to beg her to be allowed to come the next day, during her lunch break.

He just stood there, the receiver still in his hand. There had been nothing to show that it was *her*. He could understand her sounding so cool: of course, she had been surrounded by colleagues, there was no way she could speak freely. But why hadn't she wanted him to come?

HE ALMOST DIDN'T RECOGNIZE her; she seemed dressed for a play he had nothing to do with: a woman's suit, high heels, a necklace, even a little hat. She asked whether the trip had gone well. He said yes, and didn't know what else to say, then said something about how ladylike she looked, which he immediately regretted. It felt just like the phone call. So far from Ostend she was as

152

uncomfortable as he was, so he gave her the picture right away. But that the sand in the envelope was sand he had found in his trunks after their swim was something he didn't dare to tell her anymore. She barely looked at what he'd written on the back, and stuffed the photo in her bag.

She had forty-five minutes; she suggested they go downtown to a sidewalk café, and climbed on the back of his moped. The arm around his waist he'd been imagining during the whole ride up didn't appear; he felt her hands held carefully at his sides. Along the way she seemed to have changed her mind, because she suddenly asked him to stop at the entrance to a little park. Beside each other, away from each other, they walked along the gravel to a bench and sat down.

He almost felt like crying. There was something wrong, it was like she'd sent a twin sister who knew nothing. But suddenly she threw her arms around him and pressed herself against him, so wildly that her little hat fell to the ground.

'Is something the matter?' he asked, once he was able to breathe again.

'Yes.'

'What?'

'The matter is that I love you.'

They laughed; they were the couple in the photo after

all. Of course she was confused – a twenty-year-old secretary who already knew what she'd do with her life, and who was now suddenly the woman of a seventeen-year-old boy.

She had him bring her back to the spot where they'd met, one street down from her office, and explained to him the quickest way to get out of Brussels.

'See you on Saturday,' he said.

'Till Saturday!'

He'd started his moped and was about to drive off when she pulled an envelope out of her purse. Her eyes didn't meet his, on her top lip were little pinpoints of sweat. He had to promise that he wouldn't open the envelope until he got to Ostend.

He promised, kissed her again, and drove off. At the corner he looked back. She was still standing there, in the same pose, and he turned back for a last kiss.

When he got to the corner again and looked around, she was no longer there.

14

'YOU'RE CRAZY,' he said. He picked up his book, and the letter with the date landed on the little table with their glasses, like it was the TV guide – but he knew he was staying too. And in the evening they walked together to the river, glasses of wine in hand. The moon was only a sliver, and in the light of the stars the Yorty moved past them, quiet and dark, like a breathing asphalt road. The trees rustled with an unbelievable rustling that would now disappear; rustling of trees the way he heard it now would never be again.

He took her hand: a gesture of overwhelming intimacy, an 'I will', a complete surrender. And he said it.

As a boy she had used him and humiliated him, she had abducted and blackmailed him and held him prisoner, she was an exploiter and a murderess and she wasn't his type, but it didn't matter. One woman in your life could be worth dying for, and he could make her that woman – by dying with her.

DURING THE FIRST FEW days after their decision they avoided each other's glance, like long-time colleagues who have accidentally ended up in bed together after an office party and can't quite find a new way to act.

Suicide! He had always thought he would be too cowardly and too curious for that, too limited for something so inflated. A boy in his class had done it when they were fifteen, a boy for whom it hadn't been enough to give away cigarettes from packs, but who gave away packs from cartons. A loudmouth, for whom only the biggest brag remained.

Wasn't it defeat then, to elevate that moment of being stunned at seventeen to the decisive moment of his life? What had that life come to that he was willing to sacrifice it for that one day, thirty years ago? Did this make him a case of 'arrested development' or something? But if so, wasn't that actually beautiful? Did you have to go on developing and developing, becoming a different, wiser person each time? Wasn't it really courageous and wonderful to stop somewhere and *be* something, even if that was a child?

This was what the semi-slumber of the last few weeks had heralded: a euphoria, a gaiety mixed with fear, like the first days of their trip. Together they picked out a spot in the woods where they would camp after the deadline given in the eviction notice – they couldn't stay at the house; someone would be sure to check whether Fort Madness was really empty. The days became filled with hours, the hours with minutes. He was amazed by the diligent beating of his stupid heart, by his dreams which, like the string quartet on the sinking *Titanic*, went on with their standard repertoire. Five weeks to go, four, eternity and flash in one. No plans, no expectations, no worries anymore! Nothing left to go wrong, nothing left to do for some other reason, everything only for what it was itself. The freedom they'd laid hold of! – it was as though he was tricking some power on high by simply making the rules go away, by achieving a carefreeness that was not meant to be.

He wouldn't even write a farewell note; there was nothing outside Fort Madness.

With an awe that bounced back off her, because she must view him that way too, he viewed Monique: a person who knew that in a few weeks she would no longer be alive, and who simply went on living. The gall that took! The same gall with which she'd set up her entire life, and in which he was now her equal! Their love life was new and exciting, for the first time something that had nothing to do with Ostend. She was gentler, no longer so emphatically young, finally fifty at last, unresentfully pleased with what he had kept from her for so long. He regretted the doubt with which he'd ruined their wonderful trip, the small-mindedness that had made him find her bird book gaudy.

She'd been willing to commit a murder just to keep him with her; that was the kind of despair to which he'd driven her!

MONIQUE WAS IN THE kitchen, Jacques was on the couch leafing through some magazines, when he glanced up at the television that was on with the sound off, as usual, and saw Sonja.

It was like having a train hit him full in the chest.

It wasn't a photo: she was moving, speaking, with the Sydney Opera House in the background.

Her hair was different, she was wearing a blouse he didn't recognize, she looked good, serious but cheerful, a bit older, more grown up. She was in Australia! She was looking for him, she still loved him! He searched desperately for the remote, afraid of missing even a single image, but he couldn't find it, and could only watch helplessly as Sonja's lips moved.

Suddenly she spoke straight into the camera. He shivered: she was making an appeal, directly to him! And he couldn't hear what she was saying! Eyes open wide, without breathing, he looked at her. Finally her story was finished, the camera zoomed back, she stood there for a moment, her head tilted slightly and smiling, a tuft of hair moved in the wind, a sailboat sailed by – next item.

WHEN HE AWOKE, Jacques was surprised he'd slept. The clock radio said 02:30, precisely as planned. A good sign.

He moved carefully. Monique rolled over toward him, her face lit by the glow of the radio dial. She gnashed her teeth, and Jacques held his breath – but she slept on. He gathered his clothes, tiptoed to the kitchen and dressed. He filled his backpack with food and went outside. It was raining gently, there was no star, no moon in sight. He hurried to the outbuilding, found his flashlight, his money and the passports, and ran down the hill. Only when he got to the river did he look back – the house was already out of sight.

He rowed to the other side and looked in the Holden. In the ignition, there were no keys.

SYDNEY WAS A THOUSAND kilometers away, but even though he had no idea exactly where he was or how to find the highway, he would get there, with a little luck this same day. Soon he was past the telegraph pole, past the furthest point he'd ever been on his walks. There were no signs, and at crossings and forks in the road he took a chance on the broadest way, but one time he had to double back for kilometers and wade back through three small rivers when the path ended at a cluster of fallen walls. Still, he was getting closer to civilization: an animal that made him jump turned out, in the beam of his flashlight, to be a fleeing chicken; dark shapes which rose stiffly at his approach, like old people from lounge chairs, were cows.

It grew light, but the sky was such a thick gray that he couldn't use the sun to get his bearings. He walked quickly. Away from Fort Madness! Back to life, no matter how much time he'd have to spend in prison. He saw Monique, awakened by the absence of his warmth in bed. What would she do? He didn't care; this was her payback. He had awoken from the euphoria just in time to see what her plan meant. *She* was the one who couldn't go anywhere, and because she didn't want to be alone at the end, *his* life had to be finished too. She had been using him, from start to finish.

After seven hours, the rainwater running over his bare skin despite the poncho made from a garbage bag he'd found along the way, he got a ride from the first car he saw, a rickety old pickup. The driver was visibly unconvinced by his story about having lost his way during a walk in the dark, but asked no further. Jacques found out that he had covered twenty kilometers, in the wrong direction.

Three hours and three cars later he was in Strobe. The driver dropped him at a triumphal arch that was painted with grapes and apples, and bore the announcement that the Apple & Grape Festival was going on. He entered the main street, lined with a thin hedge of people along both sides, yellow and orange in plastic raincoats and hats, waiting for the big parade.

He walked on behind the hedge and saw eyes turn on him, a soaked tramp in his homemade raincoat. At the Safeway he stopped and looked; this was where Monique had done their shopping. He knew he had to go on, that it was dangerous to let himself be looked at this way, but he couldn't just leave all these people behind; and along with them, he waited for the parade. And when it came he clapped along for the bagpipers, the brass bands marching past like columns of brightly colored beetles, the bunch of grapes on wheels with a little girl inside each grape. He could barely fight back his tears at the love with which the costumes had been thought up, the tassels in the stockings of the Scottish Highlanders, the apple he was given by a girl in the parade, the earnestness of the bowlers on the float from the Strobe Bowling Club, the thought that last night they might all have seen Sonja too.

★　　★　　★

AT THE OTHER END of Strobe was another arch with apples and grapes. He waited there for fifteen minutes, but no cars left town. So he walked on, and soon found himself on a clay road across bare flats. Occasionally, through the grayness of the downpour, he saw the headlights of an approaching car. He felt the lukewarm rain all over his body now, and he had stopped walking around puddles. He wouldn't make it to Sydney today anymore, but he wasn't afraid: he would be there tomorrow at the latest. There he would go to a newspaper and, in exchange for a meeting with Sonja, he would grant them an interview. To hold her in his arms for one minute . . . it would be worth everything that followed. She must still be there; the interview at the Opera House had been shot only yesterday. And then? Maybe she'd stay in Australia, find a job, visit him in prison until they could go home together.

The afternoon was almost over. Two, three cars went by without picking up the wet mutt he had become. He was soaked so badly that he felt he was going to fall apart in flakes, like wet cardboard, and be absorbed without a trace into the clay.

He heard a car behind him. He stopped and held up his hand. And this car, gray as the curtain of rain it emerged from, pulled over and stopped beside him. The door on the passenger side opened, and Monique pointed her pistol at him.

'Get in, or I'll kill you,' she said.

Fear brushed coldly down his bones; he saw the will in her eyes. One wrong breath, and she would shoot.

He climbed in.

She turned, began driving back toward Strobe, steering with one hand, the other on her knee, wrapped around the butt of the pistol.

'Let me go,' Jacques said. 'I want to go home.'

'Asshole. Coward. Running away in the middle of the night. You don't have the guts.'

'I do have the guts. I just don't want to. Please. I still have something to go home to. If you don't, that's not my fault.'

'It *is* your fault. I lost my money because of you. And you have nothing to go back to. Yeah, twenty years behind bars.'

Those twenty years stunned him, as if he heard a judge passing sentence.

'*You* killed Eileen.'

'Did I? That's not the way I remember it, Jack.' She shook her head with a bitter laugh. 'We were there together.'

'In Ostend we were together. But that was a lie, a joke, to play a trick on Christa. You were pretending.'

'Yes, I was. But I was pretending that I was pretending. I was in love with you. I couldn't use you, so I kicked you away as hard as I could.'

'You weren't in love with me. You're still lying. You need me, you use me, you're the most disgusting fucking bitch I've ever met in my life.' He let his indignation thunder on, furious, extra furious because he couldn't come up with any better insults, and at the same time relishing his own nerve, so close to this pistol.

'You don't know anything,' Monique said. 'Christa and I were in the train. We were twenty. I still remember everything. You want to know what she was wearing? A checkered dress, gray and white. She showed me your picture, and I wanted you right away. I've never stopped thinking about you.'

She pounded her fist on the wheel. The pistol lay loose in her lap for a moment, and Jacques pushed her, dove over and tried to grab it. It fell to the floor and the car skidded, ran off the road and spun through the mud, full of screaming and cursing, the screeching of the engine, body parts pounding against each other and the walls of the car groaning.

I'm fighting for my life, Jacques thought, and he struck blindly, with all his hatred. Halfway he noticed that they had fallen outside, because now they were rolling through the mud, wrestling and punching wildly. He wanted to hit her head, to pound it to powder with his hand, like a chalk skeleton; he tasted blood and mud, clothes tore, and he felt a razor-sharp pain that only stopped once he'd hit her on the nose with all his might, and he thought: this is the most intimate thing we've ever done.

Suddenly there was an explosion, and he was free of her. A few meters away she was sitting in the mud, arms and legs spread, as if she'd just come down off a sliding board. In front of her was the pistol. She grabbed it and scrambled to her feet.

Panting, they stood across from each other, her face was covered with mud and blood.

'Come with me,' she said.

'No.' He looked at the pistol in her hand.

'No?'

'No.'

She pointed it at him, but a smile appeared on her face, and she shrugged.

'No?' she said. 'Too bad.' She laughed a little laugh, put the pistol to the side of her head, and fired.

HE DROVE FOR TWO minutes, stopped, thought, then turned back, but couldn't find her. When he was sure he'd gone past her, he turned again, and now he saw her in the field, covered with mud like an abandoned plow.

He stopped beside her. With all the mud you couldn't see a wound, but you saw from everything that she was dead, the way she lay there, the way absolutely nothing about her moved. He wasn't afraid, this was still part of it, picking up her body under the arms, dragging her through the mud, lifting her into the car.

She seemed glued to the earth, but he got her in, on to the floor behind the front seat, her head half upright against the door. A few kilometers further he stopped in some woods, at a kind of bay amid the trees. He pulled her out of the car again, dragged her up a ways into the trees, and drove away.

Just before six he arrived at a little town. He bought dry clothes, stared at silently and suspiciously by the people in the shop. At a gas station he washed the mud from his face and hands, went into the toilet and put on his dry things. It was dark by the time he reached the big road to Sydney; on the first sign it was still 872 kilometers. He was planning to drive all night, but when he started popping up out of what seemed to be dreams, he stopped at a motel.

When he awoke he felt pain all over his body, lots of different pains from which he could choose one, so he wouldn't have to feel the others. It was six o'clock. He was so stiff that he could hardly get out of bed, and on his upper arm, on the left side, he discovered a deep bite, two rows of opposing tooth marks. He got in the car and drove on. The rain had stopped.

When he stopped for gas again, he went into the little restaurant beside the station for something to eat. He bought a newspaper, and saw Sonja. She was wearing the same blouse, her hair was as it had been on TV, and in the background was the Opera House. She called on him to accept responsibility for the murder of Eileen Miller, and to turn himself in. What he had done to her, and to all his friends, 'he can only make up for by actually being what he let us think he was: dead.'

BY SEVEN THAT EVENING he was back in Strobe. It was already growing dark; the sky was still gray. He had trouble finding the street along which he had walked out of town; the arches had been taken down. Unexpectedly, he recognized the Safeway, and following that street he arrived at the spot where the arch must have been, and after that the field of clay, but not the woods where he had taken Monique. He turned, took a side road that looked familiar and actually did lead to woods, but he couldn't find the bay in the trees where he had stopped. He drove back and forth a few times without finding the spot, and when he gave up and drove back out of the woods, he found himself on a road with telegraph poles where he had never been before.

He had to start all over again. He was completely exhausted, but he was going to keep at it until he had found her and was back with her at Fort Madness.

Along pitch-dark roads he finally found Strobe again, the Safeway, the spot where the Apple & Grape arch had stood, the field of clay. He tried a side road, drove back, took another, and suddenly in the beams of his head-lights the branches hung, the puddles lay the way he remembered. He found the bay in the trees, pulled off the road and got out.

He used his flashlight to search the row of trees, but suddenly it was as though the glow of his light grew magically. He looked around: it was the headlamps of a car stopping close by. He turned off his light. A door slammed, he heard voices, the beams of lanterns searched among the trees and blinded him.

'Freeze!' a voice said.

He put his hands in the air and began picking his way toward the light. The beams stopped shining in his eyes, and he saw two men. They were in uniform, and their car said POLICE.

'She's here,' he said.

'Who's here?'

'Madame Twenty. She has to be here. I've been looking for her the whole time, but I can't find her. I'm Jacques Bekker, the Dutch quizmaster.'

He was put in the back of the car, the policemen called for backup, and when assistance arrived and his directions had led them to Monique's body, he was taken to Strobe. The whole way there, as the policemen told the assembled press later that evening, he had kept repeating that he was a coward who had missed his chance forever.

15

'I'M SORRY': that much had to be on it anyway. She let Brenda Lee sing in her mind, in search of something else she could use. 'I was too blind to see . . . I hurt you . . .' did that have anything to do with it? She wasn't blind at all, *he* was blind. Just plain 'I'm sorry' would be best. She felt the way he had moved against her, that afternoon in the Saskatchewan, before he took her to the train. He didn't know anything, she knew everything. 'See you on Saturday!' he'd shouted on the platform, and she had said: 'Till Saturday!' Never for a moment had he imagined that he had a whole lifetime in front of him without a single Saturday with her. Anyway, it was Tuesday today, so that wouldn't change. Nothing could have stopped him from bringing the photo, three hours up, three hours back on his moped.

On Saturday she would see Christa. Then she would

show Christa the photo. She hoped it was a good one —
fifteen minutes from now she would have it.

In front of her lay the photo she'd been planning to
mail to *him*, but that she would now give him. Christa
and her, the two of them, laughing, girlfriends. At one
swoop he would know everything; it had been rigged, a
joke. She still had to write something on it, but what?
What she was doing was mean and cowardly, but it
would teach him a good lesson: never trust anyone.
Besides, it was his own fault. She'd done her best to give
herself away, but he hadn't wanted to see. She had called
him Jack, and he'd believed it was a coincidence, she had
let him tell her about Christa — he hadn't seen a thing.

Nicole was standing beside her: wasn't that letter for
Brice finished yet?

There you had it: now she'd been accused of something that could look like laziness, because of him. The
trouble he'd gotten her into yesterday by calling! She
typed the letter quickly and brought it herself, and when
she got back to her desk she picked up the photo and
wrote on the back: *It was a joke. I'm sorry. Monique.* There.
A waste of time to think very long about a thing like that.
She put the photo in an envelope, licked and sealed it.

AT TWELVE O'CLOCK SHE took her coat and hat from the
coatrack and went outside. And back in again; she'd

forgotten the envelope. She stood there with it in her hand for a moment, tore it open and put the picture back in her drawer. On a piece of paper she wrote: *It was a joke. I'm sorry. Monique*, and put that in a new envelope.

She had told him not to come to the office, but to meet her two streets further along; she didn't even want to think about Brice, or Bachwasser himself, or anyone else from Camita seeing her with that child. A seventeen-year-old boy! She walked quickly, it was sunny, the trashcans cast shadows. She was actually dressed too formally. But this way he would see what she was.

He was standing on the agreed corner, leaning against his moped, his hair standing out in all directions, the way it must have been blown between Ostend and Brussels. And suddenly it was as if she saw a shell around him, a shell of helpless not-knowing, and she wanted to be in there, with him.

'Monique!' he said, but for a moment it looked as though he didn't recognize her in these clothes. 'Monique! I haven't seen you for such a long time!'

'Come on, Jack. Two days. Did your trip go well?'

'You look different! You look like a lady.'

'That's what I am.'

'Well, if you look like this on Saturday, I'm going to start calling you Madame Twenty.' He laughed at his own joke.

But he wasn't at ease, as if he realized only now that this couldn't simply be Ostend. They stood facing each other in silence. He handed her an envelope, some sand fell out when she opened it.

The photo was perfect. As soon as Christa saw it, she would know everything.

'How much was it?' she asked.

He laughed. 'A million. Come on! I'm not going to let you pay for it!'

'Then I'll pay for yours.'

He thought that was a good idea, and tucked her twenty-franc note into his wallet.

'Look what's on the back,' he said.

He had written: *For the Olympic Champion of diving, Tokyo 1964. You are my destiny. Jack.* She'd have to paste something over that.

What now? Half an hour to kill before she'd never see him again. She felt uneasy, so close to Camita, and suggested they go downtown. But after a few streets she saw the entrance to a park, and made him stop.

They sat down on a bench beneath a chestnut tree. In a little pond, one swan was swimming. I know Christa, she thought, he can't hear what I'm thinking. Suddenly her arms amazed her by embracing him. Her hat fell off, his whole mouth was red with her lipstick.

'I thought you were acting so strange,' he said.

'Yesterday, on the phone too. I thought something was the matter.'

'Something *is* the matter.'

'What?'

'The matter is that I love you.'

Sitting on the back, one arm around his waist, the other hand holding onto her hat, the panic came. She saw herself in the train again, after a match in Antwerp, with Christa who was showing her his picture. She had known immediately that she wanted him. And now it was six months later and she *had* him, and the last minute she'd ever see him had begun.

They were there. He stopped and put his moped on the kickstand.

And now – now that the power she had over her life was squeezed into one deed she would do or would not do, she couldn't think anymore.

He kissed her, careful not to smudge the lipstick she'd reapplied in the park, started his moped and climbed on.

'Till Saturday, my love!' he said. She heard a tick, the sound of the gear.

'Till Saturday,' she said. 'Wait, I've got something for you, too.' He turned off the engine, and she handed him her envelope. 'Don't open it until you get to Ostend, promise?'

'I promise.'

Now he drove off, but at the first corner he swerved around and rode back to her, for a last kiss.

Before he made the corner again, she had walked away. Her legs were shaking – when he had turned around and ridden back to her, she'd thought she was seeing a miracle: she could ask him to return the envelope. But once he was standing in front of her, she hadn't done it.

She had done it – something unforgivable, but then that had always been the idea. To make a choice, that was what mattered. Not whether it was the right choice – the wrong one was better, it took more strength. She could be proud of herself. She had made a move in a game she could not yet oversee, but, something told her: a decisive move.

A NOTE ON THE AUTHOR

Tim Krabbé is one of Holland's leading writers.
His many books include the cycling classic,
The Rider, The Cave and *The Vanishing*. Both
The Cave and *The Vanishing* have been filmed, the
latter twice, in Holland and the United States.

A NOTE ON THE TRANSLATOR

Sam Garrett is the translator of *The Cave, The Rider* and *The Vanishing* by Tim Krabbé, *The Gates of Damascus* by Lieve Joris and *Shadow Child* by P. F. Thomese.

THE RIDER Tim Krabbé £6.99 0 7475 5941 4

A celebration of energy, willpower, pain and humour

The Rider is simply the best evocation of a cycle race ever written. It's not a history of road racing, a hagiography of the European greats or even a factual account of the author's own amateur cycling career, although all these things feature. Instead Krabbé allows us to race with him inside his skull during a mythical Tour de Mont Aigoual – a 137-kilometre race. In the course of the race, we get to know the forceful, bumbling Lebusque, the aesthete Barthélemy, the young Turk Reilhan and the mysterious rider in the blue jersey of Cycles Goff. Krabbé battles with and against each of them, failing on the descents, shining on the climbs, suffering on the false flats as the race speeds relentlessly to its final sprint.

'It is a literary masterpiece that will still be read a hundred years from now' Leeuwarder Courant

'A great read – a great ride' Donald Antrim

To order from Bookpost PO Box 29 Douglas Isle of Man IM99 1BQ www.bookpost.co.uk email: bookshop@enterprise.net fax: 01624 837033 tel: 01624 836000

bloomsburypbks

www.bloomsbury.com/timkrabbe

THE VANISHING Tim Krabbé £6.99 0 7475 6533 3

'A story of dark obsession' *Sunday Times*

Petrol gauge broken, anxiety and tempers flaring, young lovers Rex and Saskia, heading for the South of France, pull in at a service station to refuel. The moment they stop they make up and Rex buries two coins in a crack at the base of a fence post as a secret sign of their love. Saskia goes off to buy a couple of cold drinks and vanishes. Eight years later Rex is still haunted by her. Then one day he sees scrawled in the grime of a yellow car parked outside his window the words REX YOU'RE SO SWEET and WHEN I WRITE THIS IT SHOWS THE PAIN, and the obsession burns in his blood again.

'This is horror with a modern face, revealed through finely observed details and delivered in taut, spare prose that makes panic thicken the throat … Krabbé arranges his characters as though on a chessboard and watches them reach the game's conclusion' *Guardian*

To order from Bookpost PO Box 29 Douglas Isle of Man IM99 1BQ www.bookpost.co.uk
email: bookshop@enterprise.net fax: 01624 837033 tel: 01624 836000

bloomsburypbks

www.bloomsbury.com/timkrabbe

THE CAVE Tim Krabbé £6.99 0 7475 5623 7

'A contemporary noir master' *Kirkus Reviews*

It takes a journey into the heart of darkness to discover the light

Respectable geologist Egon Wagter has always found the amoral Axel van de Graaf's charisma difficult to resist. But from their first meeting as adolescents on a field trip to Belgium, when three lives became inextricably linked in the caves of La Roche, he has never yet allowed himself to be drawn into his friend's criminal life. Instead he has kept his independence, preferring to learn about Axel's exploits as a drug baron from the papers. Now his life as a family man is in tatters and the escape route offered by an expedition to South America lacks only $40,000 to become a reality. So here he is, running drugs for Axel far from home in a South East Asian country where the penalty for drug-running is death. But he may also be on the brink of finally understanding the secret of the cave and a lost love.

'A diamond of a book – perfectly proportioned, multifaceted, and containing not one wasted word' *Library Journal*

'Full of beautiful coincidences, epiphanies, turning points and roads not taken' *Los Angeles Times*

To order from Bookpost PO Box 29 Douglas Isle of Man IM99 1BQ www.bookpost.co.uk
email: bookshop@enterprise.net fax: 01624 837033 tel: 01624 836000

bloomsbury pbks

www.bloomsbury.com/timkrabbe